PUFF

Revenge of the Fiend

Sheila Lavelle was born in Gateshead, County Durham, in 1939. When she was a child she spent all her time reading anything she could get her hands on and from the age of ten began to write plays, stories and poetry.

She married in 1958 and had two sons. When her children started school she returned to the writing that had been put on hold and sold some stories to a magazine. At the same time she trained as a teacher and taught in infant schools for ten years. Sheila Lavelle gave up teaching in 1976 to write full time. Her first book, *Ursula Bear*, was published in 1977.

Sheila Lavelle now lives in a cottage near the sea in Galloway, Scotland, with her husband and two border collies. She is now also a grandmother! Her days are spent writing in the morning and walking her dogs in the afternoon.

*Other books by Sheila Lavelle*

CALAMITY WITH A FIEND
MY BEST FIEND
THE FIEND NEXT DOOR
TROUBLE WITH THE FIEND

*For younger readers*

FETCH THE SLIPPER
HARRY'S AUNT
URSULA BEAR

# Revenge of the Fiend

## Sheila Lavelle

### *Illustrated by Margaret Chamberlain*

PUFFIN BOOKS

PUFFIN BOOKS

Published by the Penguin Group
Penguin Books Ltd, 27 Wrights Lane, London W8 5TZ, England
Penguin Books USA Inc., 375 Hudson Street, New York, New York 10014, USA
Penguin Books Australia Ltd, Ringwood, Victoria, Australia
Penguin Books Canada Ltd, 10 Alcorn Avenue, Toronto, Ontario, Canada M4V 3B2
Penguin Books (NZ) Ltd, 182—190 Wairau Road, Auckland 10, New Zealand

Penguin Books Ltd, Registered Offices: Harmondsworth, Middlesex, England

First published by Hamish Hamilton Ltd 1995
Published in Puffin Books 1997
1 3 5 7 9 10 8 6 4 2

Filmset in Baskerville

Made and printed in England by Clays Ltd, St Ives plc

## Chapter One

Miss Sopwith thumped her desk so hard the classroom windows rattled.

"Well, Charlotte?" she demanded. "I'm waiting for an answer."

I blinked and looked up guiltily. I hadn't a clue what Soppy Sopwith had been going on about for at least the last ten minutes. It was the last day of the spring term and I'd been miles away, dreaming of sandy beaches and walks in the hills.

Miss Sopwith tapped the blackboard impatiently with the long ruler she sometimes uses for poking people in the ribs when they haven't done their homework.

"Well, Charlotte?" she said again, and I gazed blankly at the blackboard, where the word 'parasites' was written in chalk. I knew I was in dead trouble because if there's one thing Miss Sopwith hates it's people keeping her waiting for an answer in class, but how could I give her an answer when I didn't even know the question?

She waited for a moment longer without saying a word. Then she put the ruler on the desk and bore down on me, her arms folded grimly and her face all scrunched up like a half-chewed caramel.

A hush fell on the class as everybody waited to see what would happen. Then I heard a sudden whisper from that fiend Angela Mitchell in the row behind.

"They live in Paris!" came the quickly-hissed words in my ear.

"They live in Paris," I blurted out hurriedly, just as Miss Sopwith arrived at my desk. I only realised what I'd said when that stupid great fool Laurence Parker gave a loud snigger and the whole class fell about laughing.

I turned round and gave Angela a reproachful look, but she didn't even notice. She was too busy giggling behind her hand with that awful Delilah Jones who treads on your toes to make you yelp and who wants to be a nurse when she grows up so she can get to stick needles in people. And I knew I should have known better than to let Angela Mitchell come to my rescue. I once described Angela in an essay as *my best fiend*, and although it was only a spelling mistake, the word fits her perfectly. My dad says she wouldn't spit on you if you were on fire.

So I got yanked out to the front of the class and made to write out on the blackboard, "Parasites live on other living things," because of course they are animals like fleas that live on other animals, or plants like mistletoe that live on other plants, and I'd really known it all along.

Then as a further punishment I had to stay behind after school and clean out the tadpole tank and put all the tadpoles in a coffee jar so Old Soppy could take them home for the Easter holidays. It took me ages because the tadpoles wriggled like mad and kept hiding in the pond weed and I only had a tiny plastic tea strainer to fish them out with. But at last I got them all.

"Thank you, Charlotte," said Miss Sopwith, as I rinsed out the tank in the classroom sink and turned it upside down to drain. "Perhaps you'll pay more attention in future. You can go now. Have a lovely holiday in Northumberland." And she actually smiled.

I smiled back, glad that I was forgiven. Then I grabbed my schoolbag from the cloakroom, slung it over my shoulder and raced out to the gate. I skidded to a halt when I got there because who should be waiting for me on the pavement outside but Angela herself. And you won't believe this but she was beaming all over her face, expecting me to be pleased to see her.

"Get lost, Angela," I scowled, starting to march past her with my nose in the air. "That was a rotten trick, making me say a stupid thing like that."

She linked her arm through mine and fell into step beside me.

"Aw, c'mon, Charlie," she wheedled, turning those big blue eyes on me and giving me that cheeky grin, the one grown-ups go all soft about because it makes her dimples show. "It was only a joke. Let's walk home together. You know we won't be seeing each other for two whole weeks."

It was true. I was going off on holiday the very next day. And the thought of escaping from Angela for two whole weeks made me so happy I couldn't sulk a minute longer.

My parents had recently bought a little cottage in Northumberland near my gran and grandad, and Angela had been dead jealous when she found out. She'd pestered like mad to be allowed to come with us for the Easter break, and I'd had an awful job not to give in.

"Why not let her come?" said my mum, who never finds fault with Angela because Angela's mum's her best friend and they live next door. "She'd be good company for you. She could share your room, and you'd be able to have lots of fun together." But I stuck to my guns and refused, because Angela's idea of fun is to put washing-up liquid in the teapot and then say it was me.

"Let's just go ourselves this time, Mum," I pleaded. "Just you and me and Dad and Daniel. Angela can come with us another time."

And in the end I'd got my own way, although I felt really mean, because Angela's dad had lost his job a few months before and they couldn't afford an Easter holiday this year. But I'd been on holiday with Angela before and it was a disaster. All she did was play fiendish tricks on people, like putting spiders in their beds and sprinkling salt in the sugar bowl, and I wasn't having any of that again, especially not near my gran.

So I can't tell you how relieved I was when

after a few days Angela suddenly stopped pestering me, and said her parents had decided they could afford a cheap self-catering holiday after all. She didn't tell me where they were going and I didn't ask. It was enough that she wasn't coming with me, and I could look forward to two lovely peaceful weeks, without her getting me into trouble even once.

And that's why I let Angela walk home from school with me that Friday afternoon, even after the sneaky trick she'd played on me in class. I wouldn't have been so forgiving if I'd known what she was going to get up to next.

It was Angela's suggestion that we should take a bunch of daffodils home for our mums, and I thought it was a great idea. They were selling them off cheap at the greengrocers in Edgebourne village, and we saw them on our way past, standing in big yellow bunches in buckets on the pavement outside the shop.

"Ooh, look, Charlie!" said Angela, pulling

me towards them. "They're only fifty pence a bunch. Let's get some for our mums."

I bent down to sniff them and inhale their scent. There's nothing nicer than the fresh smell of daffodils in the springtime, and I knew my mum would love some. She always gets dead excited when my dad buys her a bunch of flowers on his way home from work, and daffodils are her favourites. But I shook my head ruefully.

"I haven't got fifty pence," I said, pulling out the little knitted purse that my gran had made for me out of an old sock and counting the few coins it contained. "I've only got about twenty."

"Well, I've got at least thirty," said Angela, sorting out the loose change in her anorak pocket. "We can get a bunch between us. It's better than nothing."

So in we went and bought a nice big bunch, and Angela carried them outside in their stiff white paper cone. I expected her to divide them into two smaller bunches, but she started off down the road.

"We'll share them out later," she said airily over her shoulder, and I followed gloomily along behind, wondering if she really would.

At the end of the road she stopped at the T-junction to let me catch up.

"Come on, Charlie," she said. "Let's go home this way, through the park."

I should have known then that she was up to something, because the park isn't really on our way home. But the sun was shining and it was nice to be out, and I knew my mum wouldn't worry about me being late because she'd gone to Barlow to get her hair done for the holidays and wouldn't be home till after five.

So we turned left instead of right and went into the park. It felt warm in the shelter of the trees, and there were quite a few people strolling about in the sunshine. We walked all around the lake, and I was beginning to enjoy myself, watching the ducks on the water and looking at the pussy willow catkins all goldy-yellow against the blue sky. But it didn't last long.

We were hop-scotching down the long tarmac path through the flowerbeds when Angela suddenly stopped beside a green-painted wooden bench.

"Let's share these out now, Charlie," she said, and she unwrapped the daffodils and separated them into two little piles on the bench. There were fifteen altogether, which meant seven for me and eight for her because she'd paid the most money. And I had to admit that was fair.

"You carry both lots for a minute, Charlie," she ordered, pushing a bunch into each of my hands. "I've just had a great idea." She smoothed out the daffodil wrapping paper and rummaged in her schoolbag until she found a marker pen. Then she got to work and wrote out a notice.

I watched her warily, from a few feet away.

"What are you up to?" I asked nervously, but she only laughed.

"It's just a harmless little trick," she grinned. "I read it in a joke book I got out of the library."

She finished the notice and held it up, and I just had to laugh when I realised what it said.

"DRY PAINT," she'd written, in big black wonky letters twelve inches high.

"I bet everybody will touch the paint to see if it's true," she giggled, propping the sign against the back of the bench. "You go over there and hide behind that tree. That big one, next to the flowerbed. I'll hide in the bushes on this side of the path. Then we can watch the fun. OK, Charlie?"

She gave me a little push and then dived into some bushes nearby. I went obediently to hide behind the tree she'd pointed out. I couldn't see any harm in this trick of hers at all. So I stood there, a bunch of daffodils in each hand, and peeped out to see what would happen.

The first people to come along were two teenage boys in jeans and leather jackets. They nudged one another and hooted with laughter when they saw the sign, but they went past without touching the paint.

Next came a plump lady in a long green

coat and tightly-permed yellowish-white hair that made her head look like a cauliflower. She must have been thinking about what she was going to have for tea or whether she was going to watch Coronation Street on the telly, because she walked past without seeing the sign at all.

Then along came two posh-looking gentlemen in smart business suits and ties and rolled umbrellas and shiny black shoes. They were talking earnestly together, and at first I thought they weren't going to see the sign either. Then one of them suddenly stopped on the tarmac and leaned forward to stare in disbelief.

I couldn't help giggling as the two men walked all the way round the bench, peering hard at the paint. Then one of them put out a finger and lightly touched the back of the bench.

"It is dry, Charles," he told his friend, looking at his finger and sounding surprised. Then they walked on, deep in conversation again as if nothing unusual had happened.

I knew Angela would be chuffed to bits at the success of her trick and I expected her to dance about jubilantly after the men had gone past. I stepped out from behind the tree, and was astonished to see her bursting out of the bushes and racing like mad across the park towards the gate, her long hair flying out behind her like a flag.

"Look out, Charlie! Run!" she shouted at me over her shoulder as she went, and just then the park gardener appeared round a bend in the path, trundling an enormous wheelbarrow towards the bench.

"Oi!" he shouted furiously, when he saw me. "What d'you think you're up to?"

I looked round in case he meant somebody else, but there was nobody there but me. I dithered on the spot for a moment, wondering what on earth was the matter with the silly man. I wasn't doing anything wrong, was I?

Then my knees went all wobbly as the gardener dropped the handles of the barrow and charged at me across the tarmac in his big muddy boots.

"Leave them daffodils alone!" he bellowed, and it was only then that it hit me like a ton of bricks that I was standing there like an idiot with a bunch of daffodils in each hand, right beside a flowerbed full of them.

I gave a sort of squeak, then I flung both handfuls of daffodils into the air and fled for the gate. And I thanked my lucky stars that I was the best runner in the juniors because I flew like the wind and left the furious gardener far behind. I ran all the way home without stopping once, not even to get my breath back, which just shows how scared I was. And of course sly-cat Angela was nowhere to be seen.

My mum, just back from the hairdresser's, was taking her coat off in the kitchen when I burst in the back door and threw myself down on Daniel's rug in the corner.

"Charlie!" she exclaimed. "You'll do yourself an injury, galloping about like that. What's all the hurry?"

I didn't explain, partly because I don't like to tell tales on Angela no matter how horrible she is, and partly because my spaniel Daniel had jumped on top of me to tell me how ecstatic he was to see me and I had my arms full of wriggling furry dog.

"You're like a proper little Russian," said my dad, who was home early because of the holidays. He turned from the stove where he was putting some pizzas in the oven for tea so my mum could get on with the ironing. "Rushin' here, rushin' there, rushin' everywhere . . ."

My mum groaned at his joke like she always does because she's heard most of them before. She flapped at him with her scarf and he danced out of the way, yelping as if he was really hurt. Daniel launched himself off my lap and started to growl and worry my dad's trouser leg which made my dad yelp even more, and soon I was laughing so much I'd forgotten all about Angela and her rotten tricks.

"If you lot would just get out of the way I might be able to get on with the ironing," complained my mum, and my dad pulled me to my feet.

"Come on, bonny lass," he said. "Let's go

and do some packing. Your mum's got some pressing business to attend to . . ."

He dodged out of the kitchen as she flapped at him again, and we went upstairs to pack. And it was such a happy evening, what with all the excitement of the holiday and the packing of the suitcases and the picnic hamper and the beach ball and the cricket set and the buckets and spades and Daniel's spare food bowl and tins of Yummy Chunks and his favourite squeaky toys and his towel in case he got his paws muddy and a few of my jigsaw puzzles and books and watercolour paints and sketchpad and crayons and scissors and glue in case it rained. Then after we'd finished packing and loading up the car we had a huge pizza each with loads of melted cheese.

Northumberland is almost as far north as Scotland which makes it a very long drive, so we had to have an early night. Just before she came upstairs my mum rang Angela's mum to say goodbye. I heard her chatting in the hall, then she called up to me.

"Auntie Sally says have a good holiday,

Charlie. She says Angela wants to know if you're going to miss her?"

"Tell her yes, like a hole in the head!" I shouted back, and my mum laughed as she repeated what I'd said. It didn't occur to her for a moment that I meant every word.

We were on the motorway by eight o'clock the next morning, after getting up at the crack of dawn. All we had to do before we set off was grab a quick breakfast of muesli and fruit, give the house plants a good water, and make sure the video recorder was set to tape Mastermind, which should be called Mistressmind according to my mum.

Angela and her parents must have set off earlier still, because there was no car in their drive when we left, so we didn't even have to wave on the way past.

My dad did the first spell of driving, because now that he's passed his advanced driving test my mum can't say she's a better driver than him any more, and we had some nice music on the car radio to speed us on our way.

"I bet you don"t know what this is, Ted?"

said my mum, turning up the volume and humming the tune out loud. Since she started her Open University music course she tests him all the time on this classical stuff, and we're never allowed to listen to Radio One or Two any more. It has to be Radio Three or Classic FM.

"Yes, I do," said my dad, moving into the outside lane to overtake a string of lorries. "It's Beethoven"s Cacophony number six. I know it very well."

My mum sniffed in disgust.

"It's the Elgar Cello Concerto, actually," she said loftily. "Can't you hear the solo instrument?" And she turned the volume up a little bit more.

"It sounds like a very mellow cello," said my dad approvingly, after listening for a moment, and I giggled in the back seat.

"A yellow mellow cello, perhaps?" I said innocently, and my dad gave a great guffaw.

"No doubt played by a splendid fellow?" he suggested, winking at me in the driving mirror.

"Oh, shut up, you two!" said my mum, and my dad and I both burst out laughing at the expression on her face.

The journey took nine hours' driving time, plus an extra hour and a half for snacks and doggy walks, so it was just after half-past six in the evening when my mum drove into the village of Dunton-on-Sea and turned down a lane which ran parallel to the shore.

"This is it, Charlie," she said, stopping at a tiny whitewashed cottage at the end of the row. "Honeysuckle Cottage. What do you think?"

"It's lovely!" I said, scrambling out of the car.

It was, too. It was the weeniest place you ever saw, but it was very neat and pretty with its own front lawn and a little garden at the back and a wonderful view right across the North Sea.

My dad unlocked the door and we went in. My mum and dad had been up recently to furnish the place, but it felt a bit cold and damp inside, from being empty so long.

"I'll get the fire going before we start unpacking," said my dad. "It's getting a bit chilly." And in next to no time we had a big pile of sticks and logs blazing away in the grate.

My dad and I tramped in and out, bringing stuff in from the car while my mum found places to put it all.

"Who lives next door?" I asked, looking over the fence at a red ball lying on the lawn and wondering whether there were children.

"Nobody," said my dad. "It's a holiday let. But I saw a car in the drive as we passed. I expect there are people in for Easter."

We carried in the boxes of food last of all, and my dad gave Daniel his dinner.

"I'll cook tonight, Ted," said my mum, getting busy at the stove with garlic bread and pasta and a jar of pasta sauce. "We'll take it in turns. And Charlie can wash up."

"Right," said my dad. "I'll open a bottle of wine to celebrate."

He rummaged in the drawer among the cutlery for a minute.

"Blast!" he said crossly. "I don't think we've

brought a corkscrew. Nip next door, Charlie, and see if you can borrow one for five minutes."

"OK Dad," I said, and I went out and round the corner into next-door's gate.

I was thinking that the car in the drive looked a bit familiar as I knocked at the cottage door. But it was only when the door opened and I saw who was standing there, grinning all over her face and dancing from one foot to the other with glee, that my heart turned over and floated upside down in my chest like a dead fish.

"Surprise, surprise!" said Angela. And she flung her arms round me and gave me a great big hug.

## Chapter Two

I woke up early next morning in my bedroom in the attic and looked out of the tiny dormer window at the view. The sea sparkled in the sunshine, white gulls sailed in the sky, and I should have felt as happy as a dog with two bones, but there was a horrible sinking feeling in my stomach as if the bed were falling through a hole in the floor.

I groaned and pulled the duvet over my head as I remembered why. Angela's mum and dad had rented Daisy Cottage next door for a whole week's self-catering holiday, and I was stuck with that fiend Angela all over again.

It was Angela's mum who had planned the surprise, after finding out our holiday address from my mum. She had phoned the tourist information office for details of holiday lets in the same village, and it had been just a stroke of luck that there'd been a cottage to let right next door. All I could do was thank my guardian angel that it was only one week. If it had been two I think I'd have jumped in the sea.

Everybody seemed to think it was wonderful but me. My mum had flung her arms around Auntie Sally like a long-lost sister when the Mitchells had danced in waving the corkscrew and another bottle of wine. Even my dad had been over the moon to see Uncle Jim, thumping him on the shoulder and calling him an old slyboots and asking him if he'd had a chance to sample the local beer yet and whether he had found the nearest tennis court.

And of course they had stayed for hours. They'd shared our supper, getting through our entire supply of pasta and pasta sauce and garlic bread as well as two whole bottles of wine, and growing sillier and sillier as the evening wore on, laughing and joking and showing off like grown-ups always do when they've had a couple of drinks. As soon as I'd finished eating I sat on the windowsill behind the curtain and refused to join in, even when they started playing "I went to the market and bought a basket" which I'm very good at, even if I say it myself.

"Come on, Charlie, don't sulk," said Angela, trying to pull me out from behind the curtain. "What a face. You look like you're dying of compulsion."

But I shook her off and pretended to be gazing out of the window, even though it was pitch black outside. I wasn't sulking anyway. I was only wishing I could smack her around the face with a dead fish.

Then to make matters worse after the meal it was Angela and me who had to do all the washing up. And of course that meant I had to do most of the work myself while she just flapped the tea towel about and pretended to be doing her share.

"I hate washing up," she complained, as she dried the same plate over and over again. "Why can't we all just eat out in the evenings? What about trying that restaurant we passed just down the road?"

"Angela darling, you know we can't afford it," said Auntie Sally, cutting herself such a tiny sliver of cheese it was hardly worth the bother. "We agreed all that before we came. Dad and I do the cooking, you do the washing up. That was the bargain. Right?"

My mum brought yet more greasy plates to the sink. "Ted and I agreed the same thing with Charlie," she said approvingly. "It seems fair to me."

"You must have supper with us tomorrow night," said Uncle Jim, and my dad hooted with laughter.

"Not if you're doing the cooking, Jim," he said. "The last pizza you cooked came out of the oven like a dustbin lid. The same colour and all. We ended up using it as a frisbee."

Auntie Sally gave her tinkling little laugh. "Don't worry, I'll be giving him a hand," she said. "OK, Liz? Shall we eat with each other on alternate nights? It'll be half the hassle and twice as much fun."

"Not for you and me it won't," muttered Angela into my ear as I poured the dirty water down the sink. "Leave it to me, Charlie. I'll think of a way to put a stop to all this."

It had been nearly midnight when we'd finally got to bed, and even though I'd fallen asleep at once, worn out after the long journey, I still felt tired the next morning. Washing up was the least of my problems, I thought bitterly, thinking about my ruined holiday and punching the pillow as if it were Angela's nose.

Daniel, who'd been asleep at the foot of the bed, thought this was an invitation for him to attack the pillow too, and grabbed a corner of it in his teeth, growling and wagging his tail and shaking his head so hard that his ears flapped.

I was trying to unlock his jaws without tearing a hole in the pillow when I heard the patter of gravel on my windowpane. I looked out, and there was Angela, in her new white leggings and hand-knitted designer sweater, carrying what looked like a sketchpad and a box of crayons.

I opened the window and put my head out.

"Go away," I said. "It's only six o'clock in the morning. And anyway, I'm not very well. I'm not seeing anybody today."

I dived back into bed, but she kept on throwing gravel at the window until in the end I ran downstairs in my bare feet and let her in. My mum and dad always have a long lie-in on Sundays, especially when they're on holiday, and I knew there'd be trouble if we woke them up, so I put my finger on my lips and led her silently up the stairs to my room.

She shoved Daniel off the bed and sat cross-legged on the duvet to open the sketchpad.

"Look, Charlie," she whispered. "What do you think of that?"

"Ugh!" I said, peering at what she"d drawn

on the page. It looked like some kind of insect, black and brown and horrible, with lots of waving hairy legs.

"It's a cockroach," she giggled proudly, taking a pair of nail scissors from her pocket and beginning to cut the creature out. "I traced it from an insect book I found next door. Come on, Charlie. You're good at drawing. We're going to make hundreds more, and stick them in the kitchen cupboards in Daisy Cottage before my mum gets up."

"What for?" I said blankly, so she told me the plan.

You probably won't be surprised to hear this, but Angela's mum has got a terrible phobia about cockroaches. She doesn't like creepy-crawlies of any kind much, but cockroaches to her are the filthiest things in the world.

"She hates them," confided Angela, busy drawing round the shape of the first one to make another. "She thinks cockroaches in the cupboards are the sign of a really dirty kitchen.

And my mum wouldn't cook in a dirty kitchen if she was starving."

She selected a brown crayon and began colouring in. "And if she won't cook, we'll get to eat out. And then you and me won't have to wash up!"

The more I thought about it the more I liked the idea. I don't really mind washing up, and I often do it to help my mum and dad, but I didn't see why I should have to do Angela's share as well. If Angela's plan worked, it would get me out of that chore, at least on alternate nights. I decided it was worth a try.

"All right, I'll help," I said, laying out my own drawing pad and crayons on the dressing table and setting to work.

It didn't take long because we already had the basic shape to draw around. I filled up page after page of cockroach outlines and then started colouring them in. Angela got bored after a while and started pulling feathers out of a small hole in my pillow and tickling Daniel's nose with them to make him sneeze, but I carried on drawing and colouring and cutting out for over an hour until I had at least fifty paper cockroaches spread out on the bed.

"What do you think, Angela?" I asked her. "Do you think they're realistic enough?"

She looked over my shoulder and started to giggle as soon as she saw them.

"Wow, Charlie, they're great!" she said admiringly. "Much better than mine. I'm sure my mum will think they're real. It'll be too dark in the cupboards to see them properly, anyway. And somehow I don't think she'll want to get too close!"

Just then my bedroom door opened and there stood my mum in her dressing gown, blinking and yawning and rubbing her eyes, with her expensive new hairdo all standing on end as if she'd been watching Dracula on the telly. She grinned sleepily when she saw me with Angela.

"Hello, you two," she said. "You're up early. Playing happily together, are you? That's nice."

I jumped up and stood in front of the bed to

hide the paper cockroaches, while Angela hastily shoved some spare sheets of paper over them.

"Sorry if we woke you, Mum," I mumbled sheepishly. "We tried to be quiet."

"No, that's OK," she yawned. "It's almost half past seven. And it's too nice a morning to sleep in." She turned away to go downstairs. "I think I'll make some coffee. Want some?"

"Er . . . no, thanks, Mum," I said. "Angela and I are going out for a while. To er . . . um . . ." I felt my face start to go red.

"To take Daniel for a walk," put in Angela, who tells lies much better than I do and does it without even going pink. "It'll be lovely down on the beach."

At the word 'walk' Daniel had started to bark and yap and bounce madly up and down.

"Goodness, Charlie. Get him out before he wakes your dad," said my mum. "And don't be too long. We don't want a late breakfast as your gran's expecting us for lunch."

She went downstairs. I shot into the bathroom, flung off my pyjamas and scrambled into the T-shirt and baggy jacket and leggings I'd worn the day before.

Angela flushed the tell-tale scraps of paper down the loo. Then she collected all the cockroaches together and laid them flat inside her sketchpad.

"Are you sure your mum and dad will still be in bed?" I asked her, as I pulled on my trainers, not bothering to fasten the laces as Angela says laced-up trainers are boring. "What if they're already up?"

She looked at her watch.

"What, at half past seven in the morning?" she snorted. "Don't be stupid, Charlie. They'll be snoring till at least nine."

"Come on, then," I said. "Let's get it over with."

"Bring some glue," said Angela. "To stick the cockroaches down with. And bring a torch as well. Those cupboards really are dark."

I put a gluestick in one pocket of my jacket and a torch in the other. Then I put Daniel's lead on him and down the stairs we went and out of the back door.

There was a cool nip in the air but the sun was already beginning to feel warm, and it was lovely to smell the sea and hear the kitti-wakes crying overhead. I wished we really were going for a walk on the beach with Daniel, instead of sneaking in at the back door of Daisy Cottage like a couple of burglars about to pinch the family silver.

I tied Daniel to the handle of an old wheel-barrow in the garden in case he made a noise inside. Then Angela and I tiptoed into the kitchen. It felt cold and damp and gloomy, because the window faced west and got no morning sun. There was no sign of Angela's mum and dad, and not a sound from upstairs, so it seemed that they were still asleep.

Angela shook her sketchpad so that the paper cockroaches slipped out in a heap on the kitchen table. I gave her the gluestick, and she dabbed some on the back of one or two.

"OK, Charlie," she whispered, holding a cockroach in each hand. "Open the cupboard

33

under the sink. We'll stick the first ones in there."

We both got down on our knees on the floor in front of the cupboard. I grasped the latch and eased it open. It was dark inside, and a strange musty smell came out as soon as I opened the door.

"The torch, Charlie," hissed Angela impatiently. "Shine the torch in. I can't see what I'm doing."

I switched on the torch and shone it into the opening. And what we saw inside that cupboard made me shudder all over.

You won't believe this but they were absolutely everywhere, scuttling about on the floor and up the walls and all over the pots and pans, waving their millions of hairy little legs as they tried to get away from the bright light. Cockroaches. Real ones. Hundreds of them.

I gave a sort of gasp and clutched Angela's arm, and that's when Angela let out the most awful shriek you ever heard in your life.

"Aaaagh! Cockroaches!" she screamed, leaping back from the cupboard as if it were about to swallow her. I got such a fright that I started to scream too, even though I'm not really scared of cockroaches, and in no time there was uproar in the kitchen, what with us both shrieking our heads off and falling over each other as we tried to get out of the back door, and Daniel barking and growling and bashing the wheelbarrow against the doorposts as he tried to get in.

"Crikey! What's going on in here?" said a loud voice, and there stood Angela's dad in a short blue dressing-gown that showed his hairy knees.

Angela flung herself into his arms and gulped and sobbed for ages, making the most of all the attention, while he patted her head and wiped her eyes on his hanky and said, "There, there," and all that kind of stuff.

She kept him occupied long enough for me to destroy the evidence, anyway. I picked up all the paper cockroaches, including the ones Angela had flung on the floor in her fright, and stuffed them in my pocket with the gluestick and the torch. Then I went to unjam Daniel and his wheelbarrow from where they had got stuck in the doorway, telling him what a brave boy he was to come to my rescue.

"We only wanted to, sniff, make you a nice cup of, sniff, tea, Dad," sniffed Angela dismally, watching me from under her dad's elbow. "But the cupboards are full of, sniff, those nasty beetle things."

"Oh, no. Not cockroaches," groaned Uncle Jim. "I'll have to get some insecticide from the village shop. Your mum will have a fit." He scratched his head ruefully. "I expect we'll have to eat out after all. There's probably a cheap burger bar somewhere not too far away." He put the kettle on and pottered off back upstairs.

Angela and I ran outside into the sunshine, and less than a minute later we were racing each other past Honeysuckle Cottage and down the little sandy track towards the sea. We leapt into the air and slapped each other's palms like footballers do because our plan had worked, even if it wasn't quite the way we had expected, while Daniel barked like mad as he scampered ahead to show us the way.

## Chapter Three

We had a great time that morning, spinning pebbles into the sea to make them bounce, while Daniel dashed in and out of the waves trying to fetch them back. I got the hang of it after a few goes and managed to skip a pebble twice, but Angela couldn't do it however many times she tried. She stamped about in the water in frustration, getting her new leggings soaking wet, which made me laugh like a drain.

The sea air made me ravenous, so I was pleased when my dad came ambling along the beach a little while later to tell me that breakfast was ready.

"Oh, goody, bacon and eggs," I said gleefully. My dad always cooks breakfast on Sundays, and he does the biggest fry-up you ever saw. But not this Sunday.

"Just cereal and toast this morning, bonny lass," he told me, expertly flipping a stone so that it skipped at least six times, much to Angela's disgust. "You know what your gran's lunches are like, so we'll have to leave plenty of room." He looked round for another stone, but spotted something else instead.

"Look at this, Charlie," he said, picking it up and showing me what he'd found. "I think it's an old sheep's tooth."

"Yuck," said Angela, peering into my dad's palm. "How horrible."

I didn't think it was horrible at all. It just looked like an ordinary broken tooth, except that it was enormous, three times the size of a human one, and it was clean and bleached and white after spending years in the sea.

My dad slipped the tooth into his pocket. "I'll give it to your grandad," he said. "He likes to collect things like that."

We walked back up the lane and reached our gate just as Angela's mum was coming out of it. She was smartly dressed in a pink suit and high heeled sandals as if she was at a posh wedding instead of a cottage by the sea.

"Oh, Ted. I've just been in to tell Liz that we're infested with cockroaches," she burst out as soon as she saw my dad. "Jim's gone to get some stuff from the village shop, then we're going out for the day while it works. I expect it'll have a horrible smell." She gave a little shudder at the thought. "We'll take you out for a burger or something tonight," she went on. "I'm certainly not going to cook in that kitchen."

She gave Angela a quick hug. "Bye-bye, darling," she cooed, as if she were talking to a two-year-old. "Auntie Liz says you can spend the day with Charlie at her gran's. Daddy and

I will see you later." And she tripped away down the path next door.

I said a very rude word under my breath as I followed Angela and my dad indoors. I'd been really looking forward to seeing my gran and grandad again, and now the whole day would be ruined. Goodness only knew what tricks Angela would find to play on them.

My mum made Angela change into a pair of my old jeans when she saw how wet she was, which didn't please Angela a bit, and I had to have a bath and put clean things on as well, to look respectable for my gran. So it was mid-morning by the time we set off along the coast road, with a lovely big basket of fruit that we'd brought all the way from Edgebourne in the boot of the car.

I cheered up after a while because Angela was being as nice as anything, sitting in the back seat with me and Daniel, and asking loads of questions about my gran's house and her garden and her pets and everything, as if she were really interested.

"Well, she's got two cats called Ebeneezer

and Florence," I told her with a giggle. "They're called Eb and Flo for short."

"Oh no," Angela snorted. "That's awful."

"Tell her about the hens," prompted my dad over his shoulder, and I giggled even more.

"Oh, yes," I said. "And she's got these two lovely hens called Sam 'n' Ella."

"Good grief," said Angela with a groan. "That's even worse. Who thought of names like that?"

"My grandad," I said proudly, and Angela made a disgusted face.

"He must be just like your dad," she said, and little did she know how right she was.

"Look, Charlie, they're out in the garden," said my mum, as we drove up outside my gran's house. And there stood my gran with her hair tumbling down out of its bun and her pinny covered in flour as usual, and my grandad with his pipe stuck in his teeth and his old green gardening jacket on, and they were both waving like mad and beaming from ear to ear.

So we scrambled out of the car and there

was a lot of hugging and kissing and all the usual stuff like how are you and lovely to see you and good heavens Charlie how you've grown. When all that was over my mum and gran went into the kitchen to get on with the lunch. My grandad showed my dad round the front garden while Angela and I played with Daniel and my gran's two fat friendly tabbies on the lawn.

"Come through and see my bonny orchard, Ted," said my grandad. "You'll see a big difference since you were last here."

Angela and I followed them through a gate into a lovely little walled garden, full of daffodils and tulips growing wild in the grass, and a dozen young fruit trees just starting to come into blossom.

"It's lovely, Grandad," I said, gazing round in admiration, and Angela nodded her head in agreement.

"It's really great, Mr Ellis," she said. "You should get some pet parrots to sit in the trees."

"What was that, hinny? Pet carrots?" said my grandad, who isn't deaf at all but pretends to be so that he can make people laugh, and he grinned mischievously as Angela and I got a fit of the giggles at the very thought.

We strolled through the orchard to the vegetable patch to admire the rhubarb and the leeks that my grandad wins prizes with at shows, and then on past the hen run where Sam 'n' Ella were scratching and crooning happily in the dust. Then last of all we wandered into the flower garden which was bright with primulas and loads of other spring flowers that I didn't know the names of. When we'd seen everything we walked back towards the house, and on the way there my dad put his hand in his pocket and took out the sheep's tooth.

"Here, Dad," he said, handing it to my grandad. "Add this to your collection."

My grandad turned the tooth over curiously. Then he grinned as he wrapped it in his hanky and put it away in his pocket.

"I'll hang on to that, son," he said. "It'll be the only one I've got some day."

The smell of roast beef was drifting out of

the door when we got back to the kitchen, and after my meagre breakfast I was so hungry I could have eaten a dinosaur.

"Sit down, sit down," said my gran, pushing everybody into chairs round the table, and soon we were crammed cosily in, elbow to elbow, tucking in to Gran's delicious roast beef, Yorkshire pudding, roast potatoes, baby carrots and peas.

Nobody said anything except mmm and yum and absolutely delicious for a while. Then suddenly we all jumped as my grandad gave a great roar of agony and leapt up from the table clutching his mouth.

"Ow!" he bellowed, hopping about the kitchen in pain, and glaring furiously at my gran. "What have you put in this Yorkshire pudden, woman?" he shouted through his fingers. "I've broken me bloomin' jaw!"

He took his hanky out of his pocket, held it over his mouth and spat into it. Then he peered into the hanky and fished out a huge broken tooth, holding it up for everyone to see.

Well, you should have seen my mum's and gran's faces. They gaped at the huge tooth in astonishment, their forgotten forks halfway to their mouths, and to avoid spraying the table-cloth with half-chewed roast beef I had to swallow my mouthful of food so quickly I almost choked.

Angela kicked my ankle under the table and I gave her a quick sideways glance. She was staring hard at her plate and holding her breath, her face bright pink with her efforts not to burst out laughing.

In the end it was my dad who started to laugh first, hooting and bellowing and rocking about in his chair, and of course that set my grandad off as well. He stamped about the kitchen, mopping his eyes with his hanky and letting out such great guffaws that Eb and Flo leapt out of their basket and fled for the door. At that Angela and I could contain ourselves no longer and burst into peals of laughter too. And of course the more we laughed the more astonished my mum and gran looked, and the more astonished they looked the more we laughed, and so it went on until my face ached with laughing.

We all calmed down at last. Grandad sat back down at the table and my dad thumped him on the shoulder.

"What a card you are, Dad," he chuckled. "I only wish I'd thought of that myself."

"So do I," said Angela fervently, gazing at my grandad in admiration.

He beamed at her across the table.

"You can borrow it, if you like," he said, handing her the tooth, and she wrapped it in her paper napkin and stowed it carefully away.

My mum and gran were still mystified, so out came the story about finding the sheep's tooth on the beach. My mum wasn't at all amused, and tutted like anything, but my gran thought it was hilarious, and kept saying, "Wait until I tell my friend Winnie," during the whole of the rest of the meal.

"It's the funniest stunt he's ever pulled," she said, gazing at my grandad fondly. "And we've been married thirty-odd years."

"Aye, thirty very odd years," said my grandad mournfully, which set us off all over again.

Anyway, after large helpings of apple pie and cream everybody helped with the washing up. Everybody except Angela, that is. She disappeared off to the bathroom and didn't come back until it was finished. Then the grown-ups sat around drinking coffee and chatting, so Angela and I excused ourselves and went out into the garden to play.

"Your grandad's great," said Angela, perching herself next to Eb and Flo on the front wall and poking a blade of grass into their ears to make them twitch. "He's got a terrific sense of humour, for such an old man."

I blinked at her in surprise, for she very rarely says nice things about anybody but herself.

"He's only sixty," I said, sitting on the wall nearby. "That's not old."

Angela gave a loud snort. "Yes, it is," she said. "It's ten times older than me!"

I didn't argue with her. She's never been

very good at sums, and she hates to be corrected about anything so it's not worth the bother. I glanced idly over the wall into the road, and seeing our car out there reminded me that we hadn't brought in the basket of fruit.

"Let's get the fruit for my gran," I said, to stop Angela from tormenting the poor cats any longer, and she jumped off the wall, glad of something to do.

The boot wasn't locked, so between us we lifted the heavy basket and started carrying it towards the house.

"Charlie," said Angela, grinning wickedly at me across a bunch of grapes. "We could play a lovely trick on your grandad. Why don't we . . ."

"No!" I interrupted hastily. "Forget it. You can play tricks on anybody you like, Angela Mitchell, but not on my grandad or my gran." I glared at her, and she let go of her end of the basket so that I nearly dropped it on my foot.

"Oh, cheerful Charlie!" she sniggered sarcastically. "Don't be such a drip. It's only a bit of fun, and your grandad would love it. I know he would."

I put my hands over my ears to shut out her voice but she insisted on telling me the plan. And in spite of myself I couldn't keep my face straight when I heard it. All she wanted to do was take the fruit into the orchard and hang it from the branches of my grandad's fruit trees. It was as simple as that.

"Oh, come on, Charlie," she wheedled, shaking her fringe out of her eyes and gazing at me the way Daniel does when he's after my last Smartie. "Where's the harm? We can put bananas in the apple trees and stuff like that. Can you just imagine your grandad's face when he comes out?"

I could, and I felt myself weaken.

"All right," I said. "Let's do it." And she was so delighted to get her own way she did three cartwheels round the lawn, although how she did that after the enormous lunch she'd just eaten without being sick all over the grass beats me.

So we set to work. First I nipped back to the

car for my mum's little sewing kit she keeps in the glove compartment in case a button needs sewing on while we're away. I knew there was some black cotton in it which would be just the right thing for the job. Then Angela and I carried the basket between us into the orchard and put it on the ground.

I sat on the grass and tied a bit of thread to each piece of fruit while Angela went from tree to tree fastening them here and there among the branches. Things like bananas and grapes were easy because we just hung up the whole bunch, but it took ages to tie threads round the oranges and apples and plums some of which didn't even have stalks. But when we'd finished it was worth it, because it really did look fantastic. A little wind had got up, and the afternoon sun shone straight into the orchard lighting up the brightly-coloured fruit like fairy lights swaying in the breeze.

We finished just in time. Angela had just hung the last plum in the pear tree when we heard voices, so we grabbed the empty basket and hid behind the compost bins to watch. I couldn't wait to see my grandad's reaction, but as luck would have it, it was my mum who came into the orchard first.

"I'm looking forward to seeing these fruit trees of yours," she was saying, as she came in through the gate. "Ted says they're really doing well."

My grandad was just behind her.

"Aye, well, they're not bad," he said modestly. "I think there'll be a canny crop of fruit this year, if we don't get a late frost."

My mum took a few steps over the grass and then stopped dead.

"Good heavens! What on earth . . ." she said, staring up at an enormous bunch of purple grapes with her eyes going rounder and rounder in amazement, and I had to clamp my hand over my mouth to stop myself from giggling out loud.

My grandad looked dumbstruck. All kinds of expressions chased each other across his face, astonishment, sheer disbelief, and finally amusement, as he realized that it must be a trick.

"Well, how about that. The harvest's ready sooner than I expected," he chuckled, just as my dad came whistling in through the gate.

My dad took one look and immediately started to roar with laughter.

"Dad, you'll be the death of me," he spluttered. "Whatever will you think of next!" And it was no use my grandad protesting that he didn't know anything about it, because my dad refused to believe a word.

My mum was looking daggers at both of them, standing there with her hands on her hips, not knowing which of them to blame, and I could tell she thought they'd cooked it up between them while she and Gran were making lunch. I turned to share the joke with Angela, but she wasn't there.

I gazed all around me, perplexed, but she was nowhere to be seen. She must have crept away when I wasn't looking and sneaked out of the orchard by the other gate.

I sank down lower behind the compost bin, wondering whether I could hide the tell-tale fruit basket and the little blue sewing kit I was still clutching in my hand. I felt a right fool, I can tell you. I've been friends with Angela since I was two years old and I still fall for it every single time. The rotten toad, I thought. Here's me thinking she's being as nice as pie, and all the time she's planning to get me into trouble. And judging by the look on my mum's face, trouble wasn't far away.

"Really Ted," she snapped crossly. "I'm surprised you and your father have got nothing better to do." She put on her po-faced look like she always does when anybody plays a practical joke. "And I hope you haven't damaged that lovely fruit," she went on. "It's much too expensive to waste." Then to my relief she went stomping off back to the house, tutting and muttering and shaking her head in exasperation.

"Come on, Ted, confess," grinned my grandad, after she'd gone. "It was you, wasn't it?" And they walked all around the orchard, laughing at every tree they came to, and each accusing the other of being the culprit.

They were getting steadily nearer to my

hiding place, so I thought it was time I gave myself up. There's nothing worse than cowering in a corner knowing that any minute you're going to be caught, and I knew it was no use blaming Angela as she would be sure to deny the whole thing.

"It was me," I blurted out, jumping out from behind the compost bins when my dad was only a couple of metres away. There was dead silence for a second while they stared at me, and then they both started laughing all over again.

And you won't believe this but my dad and grandad acted like I was the star of the show. They kept saying what a great kid I was, and what a terrific idea it had been, and how they wished they'd thought of it themselves. But best of all they said there was no need for my mum to know how the fruit had got into the trees, and they helped me to collect it all together and put it back in the basket.

"Ee, our Charlie," said my grandad, shaking his head as he put in the last banana. "You really are a chip off the old block." And before leaving the orchard he picked a big bunch of lovely white tulips and presented them to me with a little mock bow, just as Angela came marching in through the gate to say that tea was ready.

I could see she was as mad as anything at the way things had turned out.

"What are they treating you like a hero for?" she hissed at me, as we made our way back to the house for scones and strawberry jam. "Didn't you tell them it was my idea?"

"I never tell tales on my friends," I told her loftily, and she gave me a look that was meant to curdle my blood on the spot.

She got her own back though, as usual, that very evening when we were having supper up the road at the North Merwick Burger Bar. My mum and dad didn't come because they weren't hungry, so in the end it was just me and Angela and Auntie Sally and Uncle Jim who went out for burgers and chips. In the middle of the meal Angela suddenly kicked me so hard under the table I nearly spilled my glass of coke.

"Watch this, Charlie," she said, her eyes lighting up with that funny greenish glow they get when she's up to some sort of mischief. And my heart sank when she took the paper napkin with the sheep's tooth in it out of her pocket and held it over her mouth.

I waited for her to leap about shouting that she'd broken her jaw, like my grandad had done. But instead, Angela suddenly gave a sort of gasp and put a hand to her throat. People at other tables nudged each other and stared as she started to cough and splutter with her face going all red and her eyes rolling in her head.

"She's choking, Jim!" cried Auntie Sally, white-faced. "Pat her on the back!"

Uncle Jim clattered to his feet but he was too late.

"Aagh!" croaked Angela. "I've swallowed it!" Then she slithered off her chair into a heap on the floor.

"Oh, lord," I said faintly. "She's swallowed the tooth!"

"Swallowed what?" cried Auntie Sally

frantically. She started to push her chair back, but Angela was already sitting up.

"It's OK, Mum," she giggled, scrambling to her feet. "It was just a crumb. I'm fine now." And she slipped back into her place as if nothing had happened, grinning gleefully as she did so, and opening her hand under the table to show me the tooth, still tucked up in its paper napkin where it had been all the time.

Sometimes I could murder her, I really could.

## Chapter Four

"**D**on't make such a pig of yourself, Charlie," said my mum, as I helped myself to my fourth slice of toast. "You'll be as sick as a dog."

We were in the kitchen having one of my dad's special Sunday morning bacon and egg and sausage and tomato breakfasts even though it was Monday. I don't know why it is that fresh air makes you hungry but my stomach was rumbling like a volcano.

It was another glorious morning, and my dad and I had already been for a walk to the village with Daniel to fetch the newspaper. The sea breeze filled our lungs and made our cheeks tingle, and it had been my dad's idea to have a race on the way back.

"Come on, Charlie. I'll race you home," he said, jogging on the spot and flapping his arms.

"Not likely," I said. "It wouldn't be fair. You're bigger than me."

"Aw, go on, Charlie. I'll give you a start," said my dad.

So I agreed, tucking the paper under my arm and walking towards the next lamppost while he stayed where he was.

I reached the lamppost and got ready to run, waiting for my dad to shout go. Nothing happened, and I was just about to turn round when . . .

"BOO!" he shouted, creeping up behind me and bellowing right in my ear so that I leapt about a hundred metres in the air, which set Daniel off barking and bouncing round me in a frenzy. I looked up at my dad reproachfully.

"What did you do that for?" I said.

"Just to give you a start," he grinned.

He went galloping down the road, with Daniel racing alongside him trying to bite his ankles, and me racing along behind him trying to hit him with the rolled-up newspaper. And I don't know whether it was the sea air or the exercise but anyway my breakfast went down so fast it hardly touched the sides.

"Oh Mum. How can a pig be as sick as a dog?" I giggled, and my mum stabbed at her fried egg as if she were poking its eyes out.

"Just slow down, that's all," she said. "You'll be tearing around on the beach with Angela in less than ten minutes. Pass the salt and pepper, please, Ted."

My dad handed them over with a fancy flourish.

"May I wish you the condiments of the seasoning, my dear," he said, and my mum groaned and hid her face behind her music magazine.

"Is there anything on the radio?" she asked, probably to shut him up, and he winked at me across the table.

"Yes," he said. "A pair of socks and half an inch of dust," and he ducked just a bit too late for my mum was quicker than him and smacked him with her magazine.

My dad was in an even dafter mood than usual, not just because he was on holiday and didn't have to go to work, but because my mum and Auntie Sally had decided to go shopping together in Newcastle all day, which meant that he could play tennis with Uncle Jim at the tennis court in the village, and maybe even have a pint or two at the pub.

It had all been arranged the night before. Charlie and Angela could have a lovely time together, everybody thought. They could play on the beach all day and have a lovely picnic, everybody thought, and if they needed anything the two dads would be just up the road. Nobody asked me what I thought. Nobody ever does.

My dad and I did the dishes together. Then I had to make my own picnic lunch while my mum shut herself in the bathroom to get dolled up for town and my dad tried to squeeze himself into last year's tennis shorts.

"I'll have to get some new ones," I heard him shouting along the landing. "These are miles too small."

"There's nothing wrong with the shorts," my mum shouted back. "It's you that's miles too big!"

But she gave a little shriek of horror when he came out of the bedroom in his baggy old jogging trousers that would have been a good fit on a rhinoceros, and she hurriedly promised to bring him a new pair of shorts from the sports shop in town.

"Get a couple of pounds of minced beef as well," he told her, when she was writing her shopping list before setting off to call for Auntie Sally. "And some of those nice big floury potatoes. I'm cooking tonight, so I think I'll make a shepherd's pie."

"And bring an enormous chocolate Easter egg for me," I added, without much hope. My mum's idea of an Easter present is two pairs of school socks or a pair of knickers from Marks and Spencers which she was going to have to buy me anyway. It's not that she's mean exactly. She just likes presents to be useful. When they're for me, that is, and not her.

Angela arrived just as my mum was leaving. She came thundering up the stairs to my room where I was sorting out my watercolour paints and brushes and sketchpad and putting them into my blue canvas bag with the cheese sandwiches and crisps and coke I was bringing for lunch.

"Paints?" she snorted in disgust, dumping her own picnic bag on the bed. "What do you want paints for on a day like this?"

"I like painting sea views," I said defensively. "What's wrong with that?"

She just shrugged her shoulders and perched herself on the windowsill to wait, idly dabbling her fingers in the jamjar of water in which I'd put the bunch of white tulips from my grandad's garden.

"Lend me that blue a minute, Charlie," she said suddenly, and before I could stop her she'd reached out and grabbed my tube of ultramarine watercolour out of the box and unscrewed the cap.

"Just an experiment," she giggled, squeezing a fat worm of blue paint into the jamjar. "I bet you've never seen blue tulips before." And she stirred the water with a pencil until it turned as blue as the sky outside my window.

"Will they turn blue?" I said, interested in spite of myself, but she only laughed as she threw the tube of paint back into the box.

"I've no idea," she said. "We'll just have to wait and see." And off she clattered down the stairs.

We'd had the beach to ourselves the day before, but this morning when we got down there we found a crowd of people milling around, about twenty of them, mostly about my gran and grandad's age. They all had walking boots and rucksacks and cameras, and a few of them had little hammers and were busy cracking open some of the smaller rocks on the shore.

"Coo, look," said Angela. "Geographists."

A thin white-haired man with a tanned face and a pointed beard and a blue sweatshirt with *Ammonite in shining armour* printed in silver on the front seemed to be the group's leader or tutor or something, because he had a clipboard with notes and maps clipped to it, and he was explaining things and pointing out items of interest to the others.

"Gather round, everybody," he called, after they'd all poked about for a while among the rocks, looking at samples and taking photographs. He stood on a big flat boulder to make himself taller, and they all clustered round while he gave them a little talk. Angela and I crept nearer to listen too, and it was very interesting, all about some extinct sea creatures called ammonites that lived between sixty-five and two hundred million years ago and whose fossilised remains can still be found today.

"This part of the coast is particularly rich in fossils," the white-haired man said. "Especially this particular beach. We'll spend the whole day here, and you should find some good examples of ammonites, like this one."

He opened his rucksack and held up a chunk of greyish rock with something that looked like a big stone caterpillar curled up in a spiral in the middle of it. Everybody went coo and wow and started scouting round the beach as if they were about to strike gold.

"They're geologists," I explained to Angela. "People who study rocks."

"I know what they are," said Angela indignantly, watching a sour-faced lady in a purple shellsuit with a nose to match who was on her knees, scrabbling among the pebbles near the tide-line. "That's what I said."

Daniel must have thought the purple lady was going to throw pebbles in the sea for him to chase, because he started to yap excitedly and run circles round her the way he does when he's expecting a game, showering her with sand in the process.

The sour-faced lady wasn't amused.

"Go away, you horrible creature!" she snapped, scrambling to her feet and glaring at Daniel as if he were something from Jurassic Park. She looked round to see who he was with, and spotted Angela looking down from the edge of the dunes.

"I say," she shouted, in a posh voice like the Queen's. "You there. Is this your filthy dorg? It's about time you learnt to keep it under control!"

Another member of the group, a youngish man with a red moustache that made him look as if he'd been eating tomato soup, was tapping with a hammer at some rocks nearby. He glanced at us in sympathy.

"I wouldn't take any notice of her," he advised. "She's a right pain in the backside. She's been getting on everybody's nerves all weekend."

But I called Daniel to me anyway and he came at once. I put his lead on and started to walk him away to the other end of the beach.

"Come on, Angela," I said. "Let's leave

them in peace." But Angela was scowling like a thunderstorm.

"What's the matter with her?" she demanded. "Who does she think she is? It's not her beach, is it? Look at her. She's got a face like a Toby-jug."

I giggled and started to pull her away.

"Oh, come on," I said. "Forget it."

But once somebody annoys Angela it's fatal. She never rests until she gets her revenge. And all that morning, while I sat in a sheltered spot among the rocks and painted a picture of the bay with the golden cliffs and the waves tumbling against the shore and the sea sparkling blue and green in the sunshine, Angela lay on her stomach in the sand, watching the sour-faced lady's comings and goings like a cat watches a bird.

At about twelve o'clock the fossil-hunters sat around on the beach to have their lunch, so Angela and I did the same. Angela peered at my thick doorstep sandwiches in disgust.

"Not cheese again, Charlie," she said, wrinkling her nose as if my sandwich were something out of the compost bin. "You always have cheese. Aren't you sick of it?"

"No," I said, breaking a bit off to share it with Daniel. "I like cheese. What are you having?"

Angela unpacked some dainty little triangles of bread with the crusts all trimmed off.

"Cucumber," she said, opening a corner to show me. "With just a tiny squeeze of lemon and some freshly-ground black pepper."

"Mm. Lovely," I said. "I bet that lot over there are having rock cakes and mineral water." I sniggered and gave her a little push. "Rock cakes, Angela. And mineral water. Get it?"

But she didn't even groan. It's not that she's thick exactly. It's just that jokes with words don't make her laugh. What makes Angela laugh is when somebody slips in a cowpat and falls flat on their face.

We finished our picnics in silence, then Angela put our bags behind a boulder in the shade. And that's when she found the strange hollow stone.

She picked it up and showed it to me. It was smooth and grey with sparkly white bits in it, about the size and shape of half a rugby ball, with a hollowed-out centre like half a hard-boiled egg without the yolk.

"Look, Charlie," she said. "What do you think this is?"

"A fossilised coconut?" I suggested with a giggle, but she didn't think that was funny either. She was staring at the stone intently, her brow furrowed in thought.

"It looks like it once had a fossil in it," she said. "Maybe it was an annie-might. Maybe it fell out, or got weathered away." She grinned suddenly and her eyes danced. "If it had an annie-might in it before," she said, "it could have an annie-might in it again!"

She grabbed our bags from behind the boulder and flung mine at me so hard it almost knocked me over.

"Come on, Charlie," she said, stuffing the heavy stone into her bag. "We're going back to the cottage. I've had an idea." And it was no use me asking what it was all about because she was already dashing off up the beach. So there wasn't much else I could do but follow.

There was no sign of our dads at either of the cottages, but Angela had the key to theirs in case it rained. She let me and Daniel in and took us straight upstairs to her room.

"Lie down, Daniel," she said, and he obediently settled down for a snooze on the rug.

"What are you looking for?" I said, as she rummaged in a chest of drawers full of books and jigsaws and games that she'd brought for wet days.

"This!" she said triumphantly. She emerged holding a box with pictures of lions and tigers and elephants on it.

"Make your own zoo," it said on the lid. "Child's modelling kit, including moulds, quick-setting modelling plaster and paints. Suitable for ages eight to ten."

I stared at her, mystified. "What do you want that for?" I said. "Surely you're not going to make a zoo?"

"Not a zoo, exactly," she giggled, tipping everything out of the box onto the bed. "Just one little animal. A little annie-might, two hundred million years old."

She shoved aside all the little rubber moulds for making lions and tigers and chimpanzees until she found the tub of modelling plaster. Then she ran across the landing to the bathroom and brought back some water in a glass.

"Don't just stand there, Charlie," she said, shoving a book into my arms. "Find a picture of an annie-might in there, while I mix the plaster. We want it to look convincing, don't we, if we're going to fool old Toby-jug face."

So that's it, I thought. She's up to one of her fiendish tricks again. I sat on her bed and watched her as she mixed the white powder and the water together into a thick paste, and I told myself that this time I wasn't going to get involved whatever happened. But my good intentions didn't last five minutes.

The book she'd given me was called *The Children's Illustrated Encyclopedia of Living Things*, and it was full of pictures of everything from anteaters to zebras. It fell open in my hands at the page with cockroaches on it.

"That's the book I traced the cockroach from," giggled Angela, looking up from her mixing. "Great, isn't it?"

"Yes," I said, closing it and put it on the bed. "But it's no good for ammonites. It's only got *living* things in it. And ammonites have all been dead for millions of years. Like dinosaurs."

I felt relieved, and a bit smug as well. This would spoil her little plan, I thought. But I was wrong.

"Look in the back, stupid," she said impatiently. "There's a whole chapter on dinosaurs and stuff. There's bound to be annie-mights in there."

I looked, and this time I found them, in a section on Living Things of the Past. A whole page of pictures of ammonites, all curled up in their fossilised spiral shells.

"Good grief," I said. "It says here that some species were up to two metres across."

Angela snorted. "I'd love to see the old bat's face if she found one of those," she said. "But we'll have to settle for something smaller."

She started filling the hollow stone with plaster, but she's hopeless at things like that. All she managed to make was a horrible mess, and my fingers itched to take over.

"Help me, Charlie," she pleaded, knowing I couldn't refuse, and before I knew what I was doing I had done it for her.

I copied the shape from one of the pictures in the book, and when the plaster was nearly dry I modelled it into a lovely spiral, using the craft knife from the zoo kit to scratch the little grooves in the creature's shell. I added a dab of grey paint just to make it look a bit weathered, and when it was finished I couldn't help feeling pleased with the result. So much for not getting involved, I told myself ruefully, as I handed it back to Angela.

"It's brilliant, Charlie," she beamed. "All we have to do now is put it where old Toby-jug face will find it. Then there'll be some fun!"

She capered about in delight, and Daniel jumped up off the rug to caper, too.

We heard voices in the kitchen, so we

quickly tidied up the mess and ran downstairs, Angela carrying the ammonite carefully in her cupped hands. Our two dads were there, and Uncle Jim was putting the kettle on.

"Hello, you two," he said. "I'm just making a bite to eat. Want something?"

"No thanks, Dad. We've had ours," said Angela, hurrying past him to the door. "We're going back to the beach now. See you later. Bye!" And out she went.

"Are you OK, Charlie?" asked my dad, giving me a sharp look as I paused on the threshold wondering whether to follow her. "Is madam behaving herself?"

This was my chance, I thought. All I had to do was say no. Then I could stay with my dad and let Angela get into mischief all on her own. It was the sensible thing to do.

But somehow it was too late for that. I was involved anyway, now that I'd already helped. And in spite of myself I couldn't wait to see whether my ammonite was good enough to make the trick work.

I turned to grin at my dad.

"Yes, Dad," I said. "I'm having a super time, thanks. We've met some geologists looking for fossils on the shore. They were having rock cakes and mineral water for lunch." And I could hear him laughing as Daniel and I ran all the way down the track through the dunes.

The fossil-hunters were well spread out along the beach by now, some still searching among the rocks and tapping with their hammers, and some in little huddles comparing the samples they had found. I spotted the purple shell-suit lady moving slowly along the cliff face, poking busily away with a trowel. And just ahead of her a few metres away, dodging from boulder to boulder to stay out of sight, was Angela.

I grabbed Daniel's collar to stop him from running down the beach, and we ducked down behind a rock to watch what happened next.

Angela glanced round to make sure nobody was looking. Then she darted out from behind her boulder, and on a low rocky outcrop near the cliff face, where the purple lady would be sure to find it, she placed the plaster ammonite in its stone.

Daniel and I ran to join her as she raced down the beach and went dancing about in the waves. We all jumped jubilantly up and down in the freezing cold water and Daniel got drenched and Angela and I got our shoes and socks soaking wet.

"Any minute now she'll find it!" crowed Angela, grabbing both my hands and dancing me round in a circle. "And I bet she'll want the whole world to know!"

She was right. A sudden shriek from near the cliffs made us turn round, and there was the purple lady, leaping about and waving her arms.

"I've found one!" she was shouting excitedly. "A beautiful ammonite! Come and see!"

The other geologists immediately dropped what they were doing and scrambled over the rocks to where she stood. Angela and I followed and stood at the back while they all gathered round and stared in amazement at the ammonite in the stone.

"It's enormous!" said a fat man in an orange T-shirt, gaping at it enviously. "It's the biggest one I've ever seen."

"May I have a look, Mrs Armstrong?" asked the tutor politely. "It's a very unusual shape." He took the stone from her and examined it curiously for a moment, turning it over and testing its weight in his hands. Then he scratched it gently with a finger nail.

"Good lord, it's a fake!" he exclaimed, holding up his finger to show flakes of plaster under the nail. He laughed and passed the ammonite round the rest of the group. "Really, Mrs Armstrong, I'm surprised at you. It's not like you to play this kind of trick."

Everybody thought it was funny except the purple lady. She reached out and snatched the stone rudely back.

"It certainly is not a fake!" she spluttered, her nose going even purpler than before. "How dare you suggest such a thing!"

The tutor shrugged his shoulders.

"I can assure you it is," he said mildly. "If

you didn't make it, then I'm afraid someone else did."

Everybody began to drift away back to their prospecting, but old sour-face refused to believe that her treasure wasn't real. She sat down on the sand, opened her rucksack and began to change out of her walking boots into a pair of shoes, leaving the precious ammonite on a ledge nearby.

"You're all jealous, that's all," she muttered sourly. "I'm taking it to the museum in North Merwick. They'll know whether it's fake or not." She yanked at her shoe-laces as if she were trying to strangle her foot.

Angela was prancing about, tickled pink at the way everything was working out. But I thought the joke had gone far enough. The poor woman would look an awful fool at the museum, and it wasn't fair.

It was up to me to do something about it. So while the purple lady was busy stowing her boots away in her rucksack I picked up the plaster ammonite, and with Daniel close behind I dashed hell for leather along the beach like a left-winger about to score a try.

But some people seem to have eyes in the backs of their heads.

"Stop her!" shrieked the purple lady, leaping to her feet and racing after me, and the chase was on. Everybody turned to gawp as I went tearing along the shore clutching the ammonite in both hands. The purple lady was hot on my heels, bellowing blue murder, and twice she nearly caught me because the tide was coming in. I had to splash through water half a metre deep and scramble over mounds of seaweed, and I would have got clean away only my foot slipped on a slimy stone and the ammonite flew over my head and smashed to bits against the rocks as down I went, flat on my face on the wet sand.

The man with the tomato soup moustache helped me up.

"Are you OK?" he asked, and I nodded, too breathless to speak. I was soaked to the skin, but apart from a bruise on my wrist I was fine. I looked round for the purple lady, and there she was, picking up the bits of broken plaster ammonite and flinging them furiously into the sea.

She never did find out who played the trick on her. She probably suspected the other geologists. They all stood around laughing while she went stomping off with a face like a bulldog chewing a wasp, and we never saw her again. I couldn't help feeling sorry for her, and I said so to Angela as we walked with Daniel back up to the cottages for tea.

"Pooh!" said Angela. "It served her right, the stupid old bat. And did you see that awful purple shellsuit? She was like mutton dressed up as beef!"

She linked her arm through mine and we sauntered on. Then I suddenly had an idea of my own.

"Race you back to the cottage?" I said. "Last one home's a rotten banana?"

"No, Charlie," she said. "You know you're a faster runner than me. You'd be sure to win."

"Don't worry. I'll give you a start," I said. "You walk up to that big thorn bush, and Daniel and I will stay here."

She set off, and I crept along behind her, my feet making no sound on the soft sandy path. She reached the thorn bush and was just turning round when . . .

"BOO!" I shouted, right in her ear, and you won't believe this but she didn't turn a hair.

"Oh, Charlie," she laughed scornfully. "That trick's ancient! Only a complete idiot would fall for that!" And she went skipping off, leaving me to plod glumly along behind.

She wasn't so gleeful that evening though, after my mum and Auntie Sally had arrived back from town and we'd all eaten huge platefuls of my dad's yummy shepherd's pie made in our biggest roasting tin and served with two paper horns sticking out of the top like Desperate Dan's cow pie in the *Dandy*. My bruised wrist had swelled up and had started looking pretty nasty, so my mum insisted on wrapping it up in an elastic bandage. And of course with an elastic bandage on my wrist I couldn't do any washing up.

Angela had to do it all herself.

# Chapter Five

It was the sound of my dad singing in the bathroom that woke me the following morning, on another blue-sky-and-sunshine day. The singing was accompanied by a load of splashing, but I could still just make out the words.

> Should a body meet a body
> Comin' through the rye, SPLASH!
> Does a body eat a body
> In a shepherd's pie? SPLASH!

I giggled sleepily and stretched my toes down the warm bed to where Daniel was sprawled out at the end. There's no need to get up yet, I told myself with a contented yawn, I'm on holiday. I was just about to turn over and doze off again when I remembered the previous night's conversation around the supper table and what had been planned for today. And I sat bolt upright, suddenly wide awake.

Grown-ups are dead clever at planning things around the supper table, have you noticed? They have a bottle of wine, and somebody mentions something in passing, and one thing leads to another, and before you can say Jammy Dodgers the whole thing's been settled. My mum's always doing it, but it was my dad who'd started it this time.

"We're not all that far from Edinburgh, you know," he said idly, pouring cream on his pudding and passing the jug to Uncle Jim. "It would be nice to drive up for the day while we're here."

Auntie Sally's eyebrows almost disappeared into her fringe.

85

"Ooh, yes! And look around the shops," she said, her posh voice coming out all wobbly at the thought.

"Good idea," agreed my mum. "And if we stayed for the evening we could go to a concert as well." My mum can't get enough concerts since she started her music course, and she's even learning to read music for the first time in her life. She can already sing the first three bars of *Nessun Dorma* without looking at the notes, and when my dad heard it he said she was really gifted and that she could get a job as the foghorn in an orchestra. My mum didn't think that was a bit funny but it made my dad laugh so much he had to have a cup of tea to recover.

Anyway, this idea of going to Edinburgh was catching on fast. Even Uncle Jim was grinning all over his face.

"We could have a meal afterwards," he beamed. "There's a great little Italian place just off Princes Street. Why don't we go tomorrow?"

"Wow, yes, let's," I said, scraping the last bits of death-by-chocolate out of my plate and licking the spoon. "We could go to the dinosaur exhibition if it's still on and . . ."

"And see a tri-carrot-tops," nodded Angela eagerly. "Me and Charlie have always wanted to see one of those. Haven't we, Charlie?"

But all four grown-ups had turned to stare at us as if our faces had turned purple and sprouted green and yellow spots.

"Oh, we weren't thinking of taking YOU," they said, and, "We'll be out till at least one o'clock in the morning," they said, and, "That's FAR too late for YOU," they said, and, "You'd be bored to death, anyway," they said. And I knew it was no use arguing because they'd already made up their minds.

Angela was scowling like a crocodile with toothache. "So what about me and Charlie and Daniel?" she demanded. "What are WE supposed to do all day and all night? We can't stay here all on our own!"

Her voice ended in a how can you possibly dooooo this to me kind of wail, and I hoped she was going to have one of her tantrums because she's really brilliant at them and nearly always ends up getting her own way. But not this time.

"You can stay at Charlie's gran's," my mum put in quickly, just as Angela was opening her mouth for another wail. "She's already suggested it, but I'll give her a ring in a minute just to check."

My mum reached out and ruffled my hair. "All right, Charlie?" she coaxed. "You and Angela spend tomorrow night at Gran's? We'll pick you up on Wednesday morning. OK?"

"OK," I mumbled gloomily, because I didn't have any choice. And Angela suddenly changed her mind about making a scene. She grinned impishly at me across the table instead, which didn't make me feel any better at all.

So that was why my dad was singing in the bathroom so early in the morning. And that was why my nice long lie-in was spoiled. I hid my head under the duvet but it was no use. My mum bustled in to my room and in no time I was washed and dressed and my over-night bag was packed and my stomach was stuffed with banana and muesli because it's quicker than bacon and eggs.

Angela turned up promptly at half-past eight, with enough luggage for a fortnight. She came straight upstairs to my room where I was trying to drag a comb through my wiry brown hair which for some reason always insists on growing upwards instead of downwards whenever I'm within a mile of the sea.

"Coo, you look like a lavatory brush," she giggled, and I couldn't argue with that because it was true.

I stuffed my comb into my bag and turned to the door, but Angela had gone to look at the jar of tulips on the windowsill. They had been standing in that blue watercolour paint for a whole day and a night, and had turned as blue as Angela's eyes.

"Wow, look, Charlie! It worked!" she crowed, lifting the tulips out and dripping blue water from their stems all over the carpet. "Get me a plastic bag, quick. I bet your grandad's never seen blue tulips before."

I gave her the old carrier bag I had packed my spare trainers in so that they wouldn't dirty the clothes in my bag. Angela slid the tulips carefully into it so that their heads were completely covered, then off we went downstairs.

My dad drove us over to my gran's because he was ready first. And of course Angela sat in the front seat of the car while I sat in the back with Daniel in case he jumped up and down and messed up her new jumper.

My grandad was in the garden near the greenhouse when we arrived, lifting the glass lid off the garden frame to let the little seedlings breathe in the sunshine. Angela quickly hid the bag of tulips under a holly bush, while my dad went to help my grandad, carrying the glass under one arm before propping it against the wall.

"Thanks, Ted," said my grandad. "Have you been suffering from that very long?"

"Suffering from what?" said my dad, puzzled.

My grandad winked at me and Angela.

"A pane under the arm," he said, and they both guffawed so loudly that my gran came out of the kitchen to see what was going on. She beamed when she saw me, and I ran to give her a hug.

"Hello, Charlie hinny," she said. "Isn't it a lovely morning? Grandad's been putting the tent up for you in the orchard. You can camp out tonight, if the weather stays fine."

Angela started to dance about as if she'd won the jackpot in the National Lottery.

"Wow, great!" she said. "And sleep in sleeping bags? And cook our supper outside, and have sausages and beans?"

"Yes, if you like," laughed my gran, and Angela grabbed me and whirled me round till I was so dizzy I almost fell over.

My dad carried my small bag and Angela's enormous great suitcase from the car and took them upstairs to my gran's spare room. There was more room there for our things than in the tent, and the twin beds had been made up in case it rained.

"Have fun, girls," said my dad, when he

came down again. "And mind you don't get the police after you for camping. You might get arrested for loitering within tent." He grinned round at us all expectantly, and everybody stared when I burst out laughing because nobody got it but me.

Daniel and I followed my dad out to the road, and he gave us both a pat on the head before getting into the car.

"Chin up, bonny lass," he said. "Don't look so glum. It's only twenty-four hours, not a life sentence. I'll pick you up tomorrow, OK?" And he drove away.

It was all right for him, I thought. It wasn't him that was going to have to spend the next twenty-four hours with Angela, wondering what she was likely to get up to next.

"Come on, Daniel," I said gloomily, when the car was completely out of sight, and we walked slowly through the garden to the orchard, where a pile of rotting seaweed lay steaming in the sun, waiting to be spread round the fruit trees as fertilizer. It was all wet and slimy and hopping with sand-fleas, and as I looked at it I suddenly had a fiendish idea of my own. Angela wasn't the only one who could play tricks on people, I decided. And a spoonful of her own medicine wouldn't do her any harm.

I joined Angela in the orchard, where a folding table and two canvas stools had already been set up beside a small tent under the trees. I ducked under the awning and parted the tent flap. A pink sleeping bag and a blue one lay neatly on the groundsheet side by side.

"What are you grinning at?" she demanded suspiciously as I came out again.

"Oh, nothing," I said. "I'm just happy, I suppose. I'll have the blue sleeping bag, OK?"

I expected her to argue, just for the sake of it, but she had other things on her mind.

"OK, if you want," she said carelessly, as if it didn't matter. "Come on, Charlie. Let's get those tulips. I've got a great idea."

So we retrieved the plastic bag from under the holly bush, and while my grandad was potting up seedlings in the greenhouse we prepared for him another little surprise. We found a stick to poke holes in the grass and we planted a charming little group of the prettiest blue tulips you ever saw, propping their droopy heads up among the white ones in the orchard as if they had been growing there all the time.

"There! Wait till your grandad sees those!" giggled Angela, stepping back to admire the effect, and I had to admit that the trick was a good one, especially as I knew how much my grandad loved a joke.

We had just finished hiding the plastic bag in the tent when my gran came through the orchard gate with a morning snack for hungry campers, lemonade and hot scones and strawberry jam. Angela ran to greet her.

"You've got a lovely garden, Mrs Ellis," she simpered, with the soppy smile she uses to make grown-ups think she's really sweet. "And some very unusual flowers. I've never seen blue tulips before. Have you, Charlie?"

My gran put the tray down on the table by the tent. "Blue tulips?" she snorted. "Don't talk daft, girl. There's no such thing."

"What are those, then?" Angela asked politely, as if she really wanted to know, and my gran went to have a closer look.

"Well, they certainly look like blue tulips," she said, after staring at them for a while. "I'll fetch Grandad. He'll know what they are."

I thought my grandad would spot the trick straight away, but he got all excited and went down on his knees to peer deep into the centres of the flowers.

"Ee, well, beggar me!" he said, baffled. "If they're not blue tulips I'll eat me woolly hat!"

I was about to laugh and tell him he'd been tricked, but Angela dug me in the ribs and dragged me away.

"Don't tell him, Charlie," she begged. "Not yet. Let him think they're real a bit longer." And I hadn't the heart to spoil her fun.

So while my gran and grandad went back to the house for coffee, arguing about whether they would find blue tulips if they looked them up in their wildflower book or whether it was a new species never seen before in the whole world, Angela and I sat at the table in the sunshine and had our early elevenses, spreading the scones with thick yummy jam and washing them down with lemonade, giggling all the time at the success of our joke.

"Take the tray back, Charlie," ordered Angela, when we'd finished all the scones and Daniel had licked up every last crumb. "I'm too full to move."

'No, you take it back,' I retorted. "I'm going to play with Daniel with the ball." And to my surprise she went.

"I'll see how those two botanists are getting on," she laughed, and for once she got the right word.

I waited until she was out of sight, then I retrieved the plastic bag and got to work. I ran across to the heap of seaweed, and it only took a minute to scoop up a bagful of slippery slimy strands. I carried the bag back to the tent, ducked with it under the awning and crawled inside. Then I opened the pink sleeping bag and tipped the seaweed into it, shaking it well down to the foot.

I was spreading the sleeping bag out again and patting it down to flatten the tell-tale hump when I heard my grandad's voice outside. I stuck my head out through the tent flap.

"Just having a snooze," I said, with an enormous yawn. "The sea air must be making me sleepy."

My grandad chuckled. "Yawning in the awning in the morning," he said, and there were more chuckles from somewhere nearby.

I crawled out of the tent and looked around in surprise. As well as my gran and grandad and Angela, there were three strangers standing in the orchard. One large fat lady with round spectacles and small beady eyes, one tall bony lady with long black hair like a witch, and a very skinny young man with a haystack of blond hair and an earring and a big expensive-looking camera.

"Come on, then, Mr Ellis," urged the bony lady, who was carrying a notebook and a magnifying glass. "Please don't keep us in suspense. Where's this new species of tulip you promised us?"

My grandad led them towards the tulips, and Angela gripped my arm.

"This is getting better and better, Charlie," she hissed into my ear. "Your grandad phoned the secretary of the local natural history society. That's the fat one over there. And she phoned her friend, the bony one, who's a wildflower expert. And she phoned the local paper, who sent a reporter. And I can't wait to see what happens next!"

I couldn't either, but it was fear and not delight that kept my eyes glued on the bony lady as she knelt down to examine the tulips with her magnifying glass. I knew she wouldn't be fooled for five seconds, and I was right.

"Well, they're definitely tulips," she said decisively. "But the colour is quite extraordinary. May I pick one to get a better look?"

My grandad was nodding and beaming and puffing his chest out with pride and importance, while the photographer dodged about clicking away. The bony lady reached out and grasped a stem, then sat back on her heels in surprise as it slipped easily out of the ground.

"That's strange," she said. "It doesn't seem to have any roots!"

She shot a suspicious look at my grandad from under her eyebrows, then she reached out again and tried another stem.

We all watched in silence as the bony lady collected all the blue tulips by simply lifting them out of the holes in the grass. Then she stood up and showed everybody the broken ends of the stalks.

"It's just a hoax," she said, shaking her head. "The tulips have been dyed, by standing the stems in ink or food colouring or something."

She turned to my grandad, who was standing there with his mouth open like a frog catching flies.

"It was a very good try, Mr Ellis," she said, smiling. "But you can't fool me. I've seen it too many times before. Flower arrangers do it all the time."

My grandma had started to laugh like

anything, gasping and wiping her eyes on her pinny and saying, "Ee, Joe, you'll be the death of me, you really will!" And it was no use my grandad protesting he didn't know anything about it, because they all thought it was just another one of his jokes. Everybody thought it was dead funny, and not one of them suspected me and Angela, except my grandad of course, and he didn't say anything at all.

The strange thing was that nobody was cross about it, not even the reporter, who'd brought his camera round for nothing. My gran invited them all to stay for lunch, and we sat outside on the patio in the sunshine, eating home-made soup and stottie cakes and pease pudden and ham and pickled onions like one big happy family. And when my gran asked my grandad for three chairs for the visitors, he shouted, "Hip hip hooray! Hip hip hooray! Hip hip hooray!" which made even Angela fall about laughing.

And you won't believe this but in the end my grandad got his photo in the paper after all. It was just after lunch when the bony lady asked if she could have a look round, because she'd heard about a secret little wild garden my grandad had where nobody was allowed to go but him. And it was there that she found the tiny brown flower that looked for all the world like a scrunched-up bit of tissue paper stuck on a twig, but which turned out to be an extremely rare orchid that everybody thought was extinct, and which made the bony lady very excited indeed.

And although I'd been dreading it, it turned out to be one of the best days of the whole holiday. The reporter was pleased to get such a good story for his newspaper, the bony lady and her friend were pleased to have discovered such a rare plant, my grandad was pleased to be the centre of attention, my grandma was pleased because she loves to see everybody happy, and Angela was pleased at the way her trick had turned out.

In fact she was so pleased that she was in a good mood all day. After everybody had gone we went down to the beach near my gran's and paddled in the sea with Daniel and made the most enormous sandcastle in the world. And when we came back my gran let us cook our own supper on a little camping stove outside the tent, even though it was starting to get dark and the evening had turned cool. We got wrapped up warmly in thick sweaters and jeans, and if you've never eaten hot sausages and bacon and baked beans straight from the pan outside in the fresh air within sight and smell of the sea you've never lived.

We were in our pyjamas and dressing-gowns, brushing our teeth in my gran's bathroom before going back out to sleep in the tent, when I suddenly remembered what I'd done to Angela's sleeping bag. I thought of what would happen when her feet touched that horrible slimy mess, and it didn't seem like such a good idea after all. Oh crumbs, I thought, she'll kill me. But it was too late to back out now.

"Race you back to the tent, Charlie?" she said, turning away from the washbasin with a grin. Before I could say anything she was off out of the door, and of course by the time I reached the tent she was already in it.

"Slowcoach!" she said. Then she kicked her shoes off, slipped her feet into the *blue* sleeping bag and snuggled contentedly down.

"Angela!" I said indignantly. "That's my sleeping bag. You said you'd have the pink one, remember?"

Angela gave a careless laugh.

"Well, I changed my mind," she said. "It doesn't make any difference, does it?"

I couldn't say it did without giving the game away.

"I suppose not," I said. "Not really."

"Goodnight, then, Charlie,' she said with a yawn. "See you in the morning. Hasn't it been a great day!"

"Yes. Wonderful," I said feebly, keeping my shoes on and sliding my feet gingerly down the pink sleeping bag towards the slimy cold wetness at the bottom.

I don't know why it is that her tricks always come off while mine hardly ever do. Sometimes life does seem very unfair.

## Chapter Six

Angela stood on the beach near my gran's the following morning, wailing and wringing her hands, the way my mum does when the washing machine breaks down and the plumber's gone to Cyprus for a fortnight.

"Help!" she cried, waving frantically at a family who had just arrived on the beach with their picnic bags and deck-chairs and buckets and spades. "Please help us! Our daddy's buried in the sand!"

I had my hanky over my eyes and was pretending to be sobbing, but it was laughter and not grief that was making my shoulders shake, for there was nothing buried in the sand except a pair of old boots.

We'd been taking Daniel for a walk after breakfast when we found the first boot lying sodden and waterlogged on the shore. We kicked it around for a while and flung it back in the sea a few times for Daniel to retrieve, until further along the beach, half-buried in the sand, I found another boot which made a matching pair.

"Charlie," said Angela, her eyes going all green and sparkly like the sea. "Do you remember last February, when it snowed, and I made you think there was a dead body buried in a snowdrift?"

I scowled and nodded my head, because I'd never been so scared in my life.

"I remember all right," I said with a shudder. "I'll never forget that red-gloved hand sticking up out of the snow!"

Angela giggled at the memory.

"Neither will I," she said, picking up the second boot and tipping sand out of it all over my feet. "Get that other boot, Charlie. We could try the same trick in the sand."

So I poured the water out of the other boot and we carried them up the beach above the tide line to where we had built that enormous sandcastle the day before.

It was still quite early in the morning and the beach was deserted. Somebody had been jumping on our castle and had spread the sand out a bit, but it didn't matter, because what we needed now was not a castle but a mound about two metres long. We didn't have spades, but we scooped and shoved the soft dry sand with our hands until Angela was satisfied that it looked the right shape.

"Gerroff, you stupid dog!" she said crossly to Daniel, who was trying to help by digging a hole in the middle of the heap with his paws. "OK, Charlie. I think that'll do. Let's have those boots."

I passed them to her and after a quick look round to make sure nobody was about she stuck the boots in the sand at one end of the mound with the toes pointing upwards. And it really did look as if somebody was buried there with his feet sticking out.

"Poor Daddy!" said Angela, doing a little war dance round the heap. "Right then, Charlie. Now all we have to do is wait." And less than ten minutes later the first family arrived on the beach. A big burly man with a squashed nose like a heavyweight boxer, a mousy worn-out-looking woman, and four kids of various sizes. As soon as she saw them Angela started her act.

"Please help us! Our daddy's buried in the sand!"

The family all turned round and stared at us for a moment. Then the father said something to the biggest boy and they dropped their belongings to come dashing towards us.

Angela flung herself down at the head of the mound.

"Daddy, Daddy!" she cried, scrabbling help-lessly with her fingers in the sand.

"What's happened?" panted the man, skidding to a halt beside her and giving the boots a horrified glance.

"It's all our fault," sobbed Angela, gulping and hiccupping and wiping her eyes on her sleeve. "Daddy let us bury him just for fun. But then this big mountain of sand collapsed over his face. He struggled at first but now he's stopped . . ."

"Gerroot the way," growled the man hastily, pushing Angela aside. And before long the man and his son were on their knees, digging away like mad and flinging the sand behind them in two great showers.

To the astonishment of the rest of the family, Angela and I turned and fled. We dashed up the beach and over the dunes and up the lane to my gran's cottage, whooping and shrieking and laughing fit to burst, with Daniel racing along behind us, barking and leaping up and trying to bite our bottoms as we ran. We didn't stop until we were back in the orchard, where my sleeping bag was flapping in the breeze on the washing line, where I'd hung it earlier on while Angela was still asleep.

"Having fun?" said my dad, sitting at our camp table drinking a mug of coffee, and looking a bit bleary-eyed after his late night. Daniel and I flung ourselves at him as if we hadn't seen him for a month, and he laughed and gave us both a cuddle at the same time.

We all helped to dismantle the tent and put everything tidily away, and my gran was dead pleased to see that I'd turned my sleeping bag inside out and hung it up to air in the sunshine.

"Good girl, Charlie hinny," she beamed, taking it off the line and rolling it up. "That was very thoughtful of you."

Angela gave me a very funny look, and I felt my face go as red as a post office van.

We thanked my gran and grandad and said our goodbyes, then my dad drove us back along the coast to Dunton-on-Sea, with me and Angela singing *Oh I Do Like To Be Beside The Seaside* at the tops of our voices, and Daniel joining in by throwing his head back and howling at the roof, and my dad groaning and clutching his head.

They had promised us a special outing today to make up for being left out of the Edinburgh trip, but when we got back both our mums were in the garden at Honeysuckle Cottage discussing the weather which had turned a bit grey.

"Perhaps we should postpone the outing until tomorrow? Would you mind very much, Charlie?" said my mum, putting her arm around me and looking doubtfully up at the sky. "Those clouds are thickening, if you ask me."

"Abtholutely thickening," agreed my dad. "The forecast said heavy rain in the north. I vote we have a quiet day." He yawned and rubbed his eyes. "I feel as rough as a badger's bottom," he said. "Sorry, bonny lass, but I'm off to read my paper upstairs." And he disappeared into the house.

It had started to rain as he spoke, so that was that. Auntie Sally took Angela off to have a bath and shampoo her hair. My mum went upstairs for a little nap which ended up lasting all the rest of the morning and most of the afternoon, and Daniel and I were left to entertain ourselves and get our own lunch.

I didn't mind a bit. It was cosy in the sitting room with the fire flickering and the rain lashing the windows, and after our lunch of peanut butter sandwiches and shortbread biscuits Daniel and I curled up together on the sofa and I read him *The House at Pooh Corner* for about the millionth time.

I had just reached the bit where Eeyore finds the Wolery when there was a bang at the back door and Angela burst in, a black dustbin bag over her head and shoulders to keep the rain off her clothes. Angela doesn't usually care a hoot whether her clothes get wet or not, but she was wearing the lovely blue silk jacket that her Auntie Beth had brought her from America, and I know she loves that jacket more than anything else she's ever owned.

"Sh!" I hissed crossly. "My mum and dad are asleep."

"So are mine," she replied. She flung the dustbin bag on the floor and draped her jacket carefully over the back of a chair, smoothing its folds lovingly with her hand. "I'm bored to death in there all on my own. I've come round specially to see you because I thought you might like to play a game."

I put my book away with a sigh.

"What sort of game?" I said suspiciously, because Angela's idea of a game is to put Bisto powder in the cocoa tin and then say it was me.

Angela grabbed the phone book off the windowsill.

"It's called the Telephone Game," she giggled. "It's great fun, Charlie. You'll like it. Me and my cousin Dominic play it all the time, when the grown-ups are busy playing bridge."

My heart sank into my socks as she told me the rules of the Telephone Game. It involved each of us picking a number at random out of the phone book, then ringing up a completely unknown person and pretending we were somebody they knew. The calls were timed with Angela's dad's stopwatch, which she'd brought with her, and the one who kept the person at the other end talking the longest was the winner.

"What about my mum's phone bill?" I objected, and Angela gave me a really disgusted look as if I was something the dog had sicked up on the carpet.

"Oh, Charlie, don't be so pathetic!" she begged. "It's only going to be a couple of local calls. That's not going to break the bank, is it?"

It didn't seem right to pester complete strangers with phone calls, but I hate Angela to think I'm pathetic. In the end I reluctantly agreed, after making her promise it really would be only two calls. Angela pranced about in delight as if the Queen had invited her to tea, and she was so pleased she even let me be the first to choose a number. She dumped the phone book in my lap and I flipped the pages backwards and forwards for a while before finally selecting a lady called Elizabeth Macadam, on Bunston 572.

"Don't tell me the name or the number, Charlie," she ordered. "Just write them down on a bit of paper." So I did as I was told. Then it was Angela's turn. She shoved me off the sofa so she could take my place, and she pored over the pages of the phone book so long I thought she'd fallen asleep.

"OK, this'll do," she said at last. "Give me a bit of paper to write this down."

I did so, and she scribbled down a name and a number and handed it to me.

"We've got to swop papers now, Charlie," she said. "Just to make sure you don't cheat by ringing somebody you already know."

I gave her my bit of paper and she gave me hers. Then she made herself comfortable with a cushion on the windowsill and picked up the phone.

"I get to make the first call, because you had first pick of the numbers," she said, and that seemed fair enough to me. I wasn't in any hurry anyway.

"Five . . . seven . . . two," murmured Angela, dialling the number. Then she grinned at me over the receiver. "It's ringing, Charlie!" she told me, so I perched myself on the windowsill next to her with the stopwatch between us.

"Now!" she breathed, as the ringing tone was cut off at the other end, and I quickly pressed the button on the watch that started the timer hand moving.

"Hello, Auntie Lizabuff," warbled Angela, lisping like a three-year-old. "It's me! I'm ringing to wish you a happy birfday!"

There was a short silence, then she giggled into the phone.

"Ooh, Auntie! Don't you recognize my voice! It's me, Sarah Jane!"

Angela held the phone briefly against my ear, and I just had time to hear a puzzled woman's voice saying, "Who? Sarah Jane who?" before she snatched it away again.

"Ooh, Auntie Lizabuff, you are naughty!" she chided. "Fancy pretending you don't know who it is! It's Sarah Jane, your sister Mary's little girl, ringing from Canada. What? You haven't got a niece called Sarah Jane? Or a sister in Canada? What? You haven't got a sister at all? What? And it isn't even your birfday? Oooh, Auntie, how could you tell such fibs?"

Angela was giggling so much by now that she had to hold the receiver at arm's length while she stuffed the corner of the cushion in her mouth. I could hear the woman's voice quacking away, sounding more and more exasperated, and demanding, "Who is this? Who is this?" over and over again.

I picked up the watch and got ready to stop the timer. I was sure Angela would put the phone down now, but she did a very clever thing.

"Who do you think it is, then?" she asked, in her normal voice, which of course made the poor woman think it was somebody she knew having a joke. And it kept her on the phone for another two whole minutes while she racked her brains for the answer and Angela went on saying, "No, it isn't Mrs Brown's daughter Emma," and, "No, it isn't Freda's grandaughter Jane," and stuff like that until finally the woman gave in.

"What? You give in?" said Angela. "All right, Mrs Gibson, I'll tell you. It's Maisy, the girl you met on holiday last year in Spain. What? You've never been to Spain? And your name isn't Mrs Gibson. Ooh, I'm awfully sorry. I must have the wrong number!"

Angela put down the receiver and fell on the floor laughing. I stopped the watch and worked out the lapsed time.

"Three minutes, twenty-seven seconds," I told her, and she threw the cushion at the ceiling in delight, which made Daniel think it was a game of rugby starting and that he could join in.

The three of us were in a scrum on the floor wrestling for possession of the cushion and the cushion was beginning to look a little worse for wear when the door opened and my mum's head appeared.

"Playing nicely together, are you?" she yawned. "That's good. Just keep the noise down a bit, could you?' And we all leapt up as if we'd been stung and sat demurely on the sofa side by side.

We waited while my mum made a tray of tea and pottered away with it upstairs.

"Go on then, Charlie," said Angela, digging me hard in the ribs. "Your turn."

I took a deep breath and picked up the phone.

"All right. What's the number?" I said, and I peered down at Angela's untidy scrawl.

"Mr Bobby?" I said. "Newbridge 9274?" Newbridge is a town about ten miles from Bunston, and I didn't know the code.

"That's right," said Angela. "And before you start complaining, the code's oh-two-four."

So I resigned myself to my fate and dialled the number, and while it rang I rehearsed in my head what I was going to say. I knew I would sound too young to be selling insurance or double-glazing, but perhaps I could pretend to have found something, a dog perhaps, and was ringing to see if it could be theirs. It would at least keep this Mr Bobby talking for a minute or two . . .

The phone was picked up at the other end and I shot a look at Angela to tell her to start the watch. She did so, then my blood froze and turned to raspberry sorbet in my veins.

"Newbridge Police Station," said a man's hearty voice in my ear. "Can I help you?"

I slammed the phone down so hard I nearly broke the receiver.

"Two seconds!" crowed Angela, immediately stopping the watch. "I won, Charlie! I won!" And she started leaping and cavorting about and dancing on the sofa as if it were a trampoline.

The rain had stopped, so I left her to her cavorting and went out into the garden with Daniel to get some fresh air.

Mr Bobby indeed. Sometimes she makes me so mad I could spit.

## Chapter Seven

Angela likes to think she's a country girl at heart, but she isn't really. She's a proper townie, who doesn't know a bull from a cow. That's how I finally managed to play a brilliant trick on *her* for a change, and this time nothing went wrong.

We didn't see each other in the evening after the Telephone Game, because the grownups had been still tired, so my mum and dad and I had a cosy time playing *Scrabble* and went to bed early. And the following morning had turned out wet and windy, so our special outing had been postponed yet again.

Angela turned up in the afternoon, when I was washing up the lunch dishes in the kitchen. She barged in through the back door in her wellies, wearing a bright red sweater and black leggings, and grinning like a chimpanzee in a tea advert. She was carrying a peace offering to sweeten me up, a whole bag of those mini Mars bars that she knows I can't resist.

"Coming for a walk, Charlie?" she asked blithely, as if the Telephone Game had never happened. "It's stopped raining and I'm sick of being stuck indoors. My mum and dad are cooking a great feast for supper tonight, so I'm staying out of the way. Just in case I get onions to chop or spaghetti to peel."

I looked at her sourly.

"I thought your mum had refused to cook in there," I said. "What about all those cockroaches?"

Angela heaved a resigned sigh.

"They've got rid of them, worse luck," she said. "And they've sprung-clean the kitchen. So I suppose you and me will have to wash up after all."

That wasn't much of a prospect, but I had to admit I did fancy a walk. The clouds had all blown away, the sun was shining again, and it was going to be a lovely afternoon. So I called Daniel and put on his lead.

"Going out, Charlie?" said my mum, coming into the kitchen with a towel round her hair. "Put your old anorak and your wellies on, sweetheart. It'll be a bit muddy out there after all that rain."

So I put on my wellies and my raggy old anorak with the frayed cuffs and torn collar and the hole in the elbow where Daniel chewed it when he was a puppy. Then we were ready to go.

"Your blue jacket's still in the sitting room where you left it," I said to Angela as we were leaving. "D'you want to wear it?"

She snorted and tossed back her hair. "Don't be stupid, Charlie!" she exclaimed. "That jacket cost nearly two hundred dollars. I don't want Daniel's muddy paws all over it. I'd rather freeze!"

We set off towards the cliff path above the bay. Angela's plan was to walk along the top of the cliffs and back through the fields for a change, as the tide was up and there wasn't much beach.

"Keep a look out for muffins," she said, peering hopefully about in the grass. "My dad says they'll be making their nests in burrows in the dunes." And of course that made me laugh so much I couldn't stay sour-faced any longer.

"Puffins, not muffins," I giggled, but she took no notice as usual, running on ahead and jumping in muddy puddles like a two-year-old.

Daniel was tugging like mad on the lead, because like all spaniels he loves splashing about in water. So after checking that there were no sheep or lambs in the fields nearby I let him run free. He chased after Angela to jump in puddles too, and in no time they were both wet and filthy all over.

It was a great walk. Daniel galloped about, poking his nose down rabbit holes and sniffing at all the country smells. Angela enjoyed herself and didn't complain once, even though there was a cool breeze blowing and she must have felt chilly without a coat. We walked about a mile around the coast, then we climbed over a stile onto a path that led through a turnip field, past Stoat's Farm, and back across the meadows to Bunston village.

We were halfway across the turnip field when I suddenly had my first great idea. Angela didn't know it, but all this land belonged to Mr Stoat, the farmer who had sold Honeysuckle Cottage to my mum and dad. I'd actually met Mr Stoat only a couple of mornings before, when I was out in the front garden with my dad. He'd stopped his pick-up truck outside our gate and leaned out of the cab in his tweed cap and sunglasses and dungarees.

"Settling in all right?" he shouted, bellowing above the noise of the engine.

My dad grinned and nodded to show that

we were, then Mr Stoat shouted something else, swivelling in his seat to point across the fields towards the farm.

My dad looked puzzled.

"What did he say, Charlie?" he muttered out of the side of his mouth. "Turn up for dinner? Surely he's not inviting us for a meal at the farm?"

I shrugged my shoulders because I hadn't quite caught it either.

"It was something like turn up for dinner," I said. "That's what it sounded like to me."

"Me too," said my dad, baffled. He turned back to Mr Stoat. "What was that, George?" he shouted. "Did you say turn up for dinner? D'you mean at the farm?"

The farmer shook his head impatiently, waving his arm again to indicate the fields.

"I said help yourselves to a TURNIP FOR DINNER!" he hollered. "From the FIELD! As many as you want!" And my dad laughed and nodded again, and gave a thumbs-up sign in reply.

I'd forgotten all about it, until seeing the

turnips growing in neat rows in the field reminded me. So I grabbed Angela's arm.

"Ooh, look, Angela," I said. "Turnips. Don't they look nice? I love turnips, mashed with loads of butter and black pepper, don't you? Shall we nick a couple to go with our supper tonight?"

Angela stopped dead and stared at me in astonishment. She's always pretending to steal things, like the necklace she said she'd pinched from the gift shop in Barlow, which turned out to have come out of a Christmas cracker, and the dog she once said she'd stolen from outside the paper shop, which she was only looking after for the day. But I don't think she's ever really stolen anything in her life.

She laughed scornfully and stood there watching me, hands on hips.

"Come off it, Charlie!" she snorted. "Steal the farmer's turnips? You? You wouldn't dare!"

"Oh, wouldn't I?" I said carelessly, as if I stole things every day of my life. And I bent over a big fat turnip and pulled it up by its roots.

"There!" I said, shaking the soil off it and testing its weight in my hands. "A couple of pounds at least."

I turned to grin at her. "Come on, Angela," I said. "One turnip's not enough for six people, and I don't fancy carrying two. You'll have to nick one as well. Unless you're scared, of course?" I added, with a sneer.

She dithered about for ages, looking apprehensively over her shoulder. I waited a moment longer, then I put my face right next to hers.

"Scaredy-cat Mitchell, scaredy-cat Mitchell," I chanted in a sing-song voice, and she gave me such a push I nearly fell over.

"That's what you think, Cleverclogs Ellis!" she retorted. "Watch this!"

I could hardly stop myself from giggling out loud when she bent down and yanked up an even bigger turnip than mine.

I shoved my turnip inside my anorak and zipped it up, which made me look as if I had a belly like Laurence Parker's.

"We'd better run, Angela," I said. "That's

the farm over there, and somebody could be looking out of the window."

She gave a little scream at that, and started to hurry through the field towards the next stile.

"Ooh, Charlie, it would be awful if we got caught," she moaned. "My mum'd kill me if she found out!"

Daniel ran ahead and leaped the stile into a grassy meadow, where half a dozen young heifers were grazing in a corner near the hedge. Angela scrambled awkwardly over after him, her turnip clutched under one arm. I followed next, and as I jumped to the ground I saw the heifers lift their heads to stare curiously at the sight of the dog.

I don't know why it is, but young cows are the nosiest creatures on earth. I've been followed by them loads of times, when I've been out for walks with my dad. So when this lot started to amble along behind us I suddenly had another great idea. I knew they were just being curious and didn't mean us any harm. But did Angela know that? And did she know

they were just young heifers and not dangerous bulls? There was only one way to find
out.

I waited until the heifers were quite close
behind us, then I gave Angela a nudge.

"Angela!" I muttered into her ear. "Don't
look now, but we're being followed by a herd
of bulls!"

And of course the first thing she did was
look round. Then her eyes went wide and she
clutched at me with her one free hand.

"Oh, lord, Charlie!" she gasped, her face
turning the colour of wallpaper paste. "What
are we gonna do now?"

"Keep calm, Angela," I urged. "Just stand
still. They might go away."

The heifers cantered nearer, then stopped to
stand in a group nearby, swishing their tails
and snorting down their noses.

"I wish you hadn't worn your red sweater,
Angela," I murmured, and Angela shrieked
and closed her eyes.

"I daren't look!" she groaned. "Are they
going to charge?"

One of the heifers said "Moo!" and pawed at the ground. Angela shrieked again.

"Listen, Angela," I said. "It's your red sweater that's making them angry. For Pete's sake take it off." I pointed at the gate at the other side of the field. "Look, why don't you head slowly for the gate? I'll distract the bulls while you escape. Then I'll follow you. OK?"

She looked at me, round-eyed. "Are you sure?" she quavered, and I pushed her away from me.

"Just do it, Angela!" I ordered, in a bossy voice like Evil Edna who works in Edgebourne library, and Angela wasted no more time.

She put her turnip down on the ground and hastily pulled the red sweater off over her head to reveal a black T-shirt underneath.

"Don't forget the turnip," I told her. "Or all this will have been for nothing."

She obediently picked up the turnip and set off across the meadow towards the gate, walking quickly with her head down.

The heifers had lost interest by now and were beginning to wander off, so I shouted at them and waved the red sweater to stir them up a bit. They kicked their heels up in the air and galloped friskily away across the grass, then they wheeled round and regrouped before galloping back towards me again.

"WHAAAH!" I roared, running to meet them and waving both arms, the way I'd seen my dad do once when some cattle got too close for comfort. And of course that got Daniel going and he started barking and jumping up and down and racing round in circles and that was too much for the heifers altogether. They rolled their eyes in alarm, then stampeded away towards the stile.

I knew they would soon calm down and return to their grazing, so I called Daniel to heel and strolled casually over to the gate.

Angela was in the lane on the other side, watching me through the bars. She tried to fling her arms round me as soon as I'd climbed over, but I pushed her off.

"Ooh, Charlie, you are brave!" she cried. "You saved my life! I'll never be horrible to you again!"

I threw her red sweater at her and started to fall about laughing.

"Get lost, Angela!" I giggled, and it was my turn to dance gleefully about for a change. "I didn't save your life at all. Those aren't bulls, stupid! They're only baby cows!"

Her mouth dropped open and her face went as red as her sweater with rage and I capered about so much that the turnip fell out of the front of my anorak and bounced out onto the ground which for some reason made me laugh even more.

Angela took a deep breath and I knew I was in for it but just then the sound of a tractor coming along the lane made us both turn round. I grabbed Daniel and put his lead on as the tractor approached. Then I saw who was driving it. The farmer, George Stoat himself.

He recognised me and leaned out to give me a cheery wave.

"I see you've helped yourself to some turnips like I said," he shouted as he rumbled by. "I hope you enjoy them!"

I grinned and waved back, then I had to duck quickly because Angela had suddenly given this awful murderous yell and flung her turnip at my head.

'Yah, you missed! What a rotten shot!" I called after her as she went stomping furiously off down the lane. And I couldn't resist capering about a bit more.

She didn't look back. All she did was to shout an extremely rude word at me over her shoulder as she went.

I watched her go, than I picked up both the turnips and started to follow her back to Bunston, my elation dwindling as I wondered what she'd do to get her revenge. It would be something really horrible this time, I felt sure.

## Chapter Eight

"Right, ladies. What's it to be?" said Uncle Jim. "Funfair or country park?"

It was ten o'clock in the morning and we were all in North Merwick bus station, peering at a timetable on the wall. Loads of people were milling about because it was Good Friday and the start of the Easter weekend.

We had found out from the timetable that there were two suitable excursions that day, one going down the coast to the Spanish City

Funfair, the other going inland to the Northumberland Country Park.

Auntie Sally, shivering in the draughty station even though she was all wrapped up as if she was going to the moon, said she didn't care where we went, and my mum didn't mind either. So it was up to Angela and me.

"What's it to be, girls?" said Uncle Jim, looking at us enquiringly.

"Funfair," said Angela at once.

"Country park," I said, a split second too late. I do like funfairs, but the rides make me as sick as a parrot and Angela knows it.

My dad took some coins from his pocket.

"We'll toss for it," he said. "Heads funfair, tails country park. OK?"

"OK," I said gloomily, because I never win at heads or tails, and my dad flipped a fifty-pence piece and caught it on the back of his hand.

"Tails!" he said, to my amazement. "Country park it is."

Uncle Jim peered again at the board. "Right

then, which bus do we get?" he said. "This is double Dutch to me."

I shot a look at Angela, expecting her to sulk, but she just grinned.

"You win, Charlie," she said good-naturedly. "The country park will be better for Daniel anyway." She smiled up at her father. "Don't worry, Dad. I'll just run and ask that bus driver over there." She patted Daniel on the head and shot off.

A man with a collecting tin and a bundle of raffle tickets came up to my dad.

"Help the Lifeboats, sir?" he said hopefully. "Buy a raffle ticket for a brand new Rover?"

My dad shook his head. "No thanks, mate. I've already got a dog," he said, looking at me to see if I'd got the joke.

I grinned feebly but it didn't cheer me up. I was watching Angela's head bobbing as she made her way through the crowd, and I had that awful squirmy feeling in my stomach, as if I'd swallowed a live snake. She hadn't once mentioned how I'd tricked her, not even the night before, when we'd had those very same turnips for supper. She'd laughed and chattered the whole evening, as friendly as anything. And after the meal she'd even done more than her share of the washing up, which only made me more uneasy than ever, because Angela is usually at her most dangerous when she's being as nice as pie.

There wasn't time to worry about it, for she was back almost at once, pushing past a fat lady with a million suitcases on a trolley.

"Come on, you lot!" she urged. "That's our bus over there! It's leaving in ten seconds!" She herded us up like Mr Stoat's sheepdog and shoved us all onto a bus which was standing facing out of the station, engine running.

We were just in time. As soon as my dad had paid the driver, the doors hissed closed. The bus pulled out of the station and we sank into three double seats near the back. The two mums sat together so they could gossip about Auntie Sally's other neighbour, who left her husband to run away with her driving instructor, and at sixty-five is old enough to know better. The two dads sat together so they could talk about football and who was likely to win the World Cup. And Daniel and I were stuck with Angela, in the seat between.

I stuffed my rucksack under the seat, then I cuddled Daniel on my lap, looking out of the window and not speaking to Angela at all. The sky was grey and cold and it looked a bit like rain, but it was the last day of the Mitchells' holiday and our last chance to have a day out together.

The bus trip had been my dad's suggestion. We couldn't all squeeze into one car, he'd pointed out, and it would be daft to go separately. We would hardly see each other at all. Uncle Jim had agreed, but my mum had looked at them suspiciously.

"It wouldn't be anything to do with not wanting to drink and drive?" she'd asked. "You're not thinking of having a few pints at the pub when we get there?" And the two dads had looked all hurt and innocent and said, "Who, us?" as if the thought had never entered their heads.

In the end the two mums had said that it

would be nice to travel together and have a cosy chat. So it was decided that we would leave both cars at the bus station, which meant that we all had to wear sweaters and waterproof anoraks in case it rained.

I was wearing my brown and cream woolly jumper that my gran had knitted me for Christmas, but I'd persuaded my mum to let me carry my anorak in my rucksack, partly because I'm ashamed of it but also because I didn't want to be muffled up like an Eskimo all day. And at the last minute I'd fetched Angela's posh blue jacket from the chair in the sitting room and put that in as well. She might want to wear it, and in any case it might be the last opportunity to give her it back. They were driving home on Saturday and wanted an early start.

Angela was humming contentedly as we went along. She was dressed warmly in a quilted waterproof coat with a hood, so she wouldn't need the blue jacket at all. Now I would have to carry it around all day, because she certainly wouldn't want to. I was stupid not to have left it in the car, but it was too late to think of that now.

The grown-ups were deep in conversation and hadn't noticed anything wrong, but as I gazed out of the bus window it began to occur to me that I could still see the sea on my left. We should have turned inland towards the Cheviot Hills long ago, if we were on the way to the Northumberland Country Park.

I turned from the window to find Angela watching me, her blue eyes dancing with mirth.

"What's that horrible face for, Charlie?" she tittered. "You look dead crabbit, like Miss Sopwith on a Monday morning."

"You ratbag!" I seethed, glaring at her. "You've got us on the wrong bus!"

She blinked in surprise, then she leaned across me to look out.

"Good heavens, Charlie!" she exclaimed. "So I have! How could that have happened?" And you won't believe this but she insisted it had been a mistake. She kneeled up on the seat to apologize first to our two dads and then to our mums, and they chuckled as if it was the funniest thing she'd ever done, even though nobody was fooled for a minute.

"What a little rascal! She'll do anything to get her own way," they said to one another, looking at the sea and shaking their heads in amusement. And nobody seemed to think it mattered very much at all.

I hugged Daniel and stroked his ears and whispered that he was my only true friend in the whole world, and we decided that neither of us would speak to Angela for the rest of the day.

I managed to keep my vow for almost the whole journey, even though she got up to all sorts of tricks to try to make me laugh. First she tried telling me silly jokes that could only have come out of the Dandy or the Beano. Then when that didn't work she started yawning noisily to make everybody else on the bus yawn. And then finally she began scratching herself all over as if she had fleas, until everyone around us was scratching as well.

A posh lady across the aisle, wearing a fur

beret that looked like a huge fat cat asleep on her head, suddenly snorted in disgust and moved to another seat, and that's when I had a fit of the giggles. And as usual once I'd started giggling I couldn't sulk any longer. In any case I felt I'd been let off quite lightly. If putting us on the wrong bus was Angela's way of settling the score, then maybe I could relax and enjoy the rest of the trip. I really should have known better, because Angela was to get her revenge not once, not twice, but three times that day.

Anyway, by the time we got off the bus at the Spanish City we were the best of friends. We spent an hour or so roaming around the funfair, and it was great. My mum and Auntie Sally went off with Daniel to have their fortunes told, just for a laugh. My dad won a big fluffy orange rabbit on the rifle range. And Uncle Jim won so many coconuts at the coconut shy that the owner refused to let him have any more goes.

As for Angela and me, we had the best time of all. We went on the dodgem cars, we had a good old scream together on the ghost train, we scoffed ice-cream and toffee apples and candy floss, and we even managed a ride on the Big Dipper without me being sick.

I was feeling as wobbly as a dead jellyfish afterwards though, so I was glad when we all met up again and my mum suggested we find somewhere to have lunch. We walked out of the funfair and along the sea front, with the grown-ups arguing about where we should go.

"The Blue Lion does a good bar lunch," said Uncle Jim, who used to be a travelling sales-man and seems to know every pub and restaur-ant in England. But my mum shook her head.

"We don't want to take the girls into a pub," she objected primly. "Let's find a nice tea-shop instead."

"What about that one over there?" said Auntie Sally, and we all crossed the road.

"Abandon hope all ye who enter here," said my dad, opening the tea-shop door. "You'll only get a tea and not a beer!" And even Auntie Sally gave a little splutter of laughter at that.

"Behave yourself, Ted," said my mum,

looking round for a table, but a waitress in a frilly apron came hurrying towards us.

"Sorry," she said, ushering us quickly out again. "No dogs."

"Never mind," said Uncle Jim. "I'm sure the Blue Lion allows dogs in the family room at the back." So the dads got their own way after all, which put them in a very good mood, and my dad hopscotched along the pavement all the way.

"Oh Lizzie dear, I'm feeling queer, lend's a quid to buy a beer," he chanted in a broad Geordie accent, as we all squeezed round a table in the bay window of the pub. Everybody took their coats off, and I shoved my rucksack and the orange rabbit under the seat. Daniel, after a drink of water and a Bonio, curled up beside them, glad of a rest.

"They do a good spaghetti here," said Uncle Jim, passing the menus round. "But they do give you rather a lot of sauce."

"Just like him!" said my mum, indicating my dad across the table, and he beamed and blew her a kiss.

It was a hilarious lunch. I've never known Auntie Sally laugh so much, but it may have been something to do with the fact that she had two glasses of white wine with her haddock and chips.

We all ordered haddock and chips, except my dad. He ordered the cod, which was a mistake, because it came in a coating of bright orange breadcrumbs that looked as if it had been dyed.

"This is the piece of cod which passeth all understanding," he intoned, after the first mouthful, and my mum gave him a kick on the shin under the table which made him yelp.

It went on like that the whole time, and even the waiter joined in the fun. My dad asked him for a toothpick halfway through the meal, and he looked surprised.

"Why don't you put them in a glass like you normally do?" he said, and Auntie Sally giggled so much she got a stitch in her side and had to have another glass of wine to recover.

I was really enjoying myself, so Angela's next horrible trick came as a complete surprise.

We had almost finished eating, and Angela had only a few chips left. The little pile of tomato sauce on the edge of her plate had all gone, so she picked up the sauce bottle and handed it to me.

"Give it a good shake for me, Charlie, will you?" she begged. "You're much better at it than me."

So I obligingly took the bottle and gave it a vigorous shake, and to my horror the cap flew off and great gouts of tomato sauce came flying out and splattered me and the table-cloth as well as everybody else round the table.

"Charlie! You stupid child!" shrieked Auntie Sally, grabbing a paper napkin as a big red blob landed on the front of her blouse.

"S . . . orry," I mumbled, putting the bottle hastily down. "The top was loose."

My mum tutted and sighed and wiped a couple of streaks off her face. My dad was peering sadly into his glass of beer where a small island of sauce was slowly sinking in the middle, and Uncle Jim was scrubbing furiously at his tie. Angela was the only one it had missed,

"Oh dear," she said, all wide-eyed and innocent. "Somebody didn't screw the top back on properly." But as she was the only one who'd had tomato sauce, I knew perfectly well who that somebody was.

Uncle Jim paid the bill and we all trooped out into the street. We stood in a group on the pavement, our happy mood spoiled.

"What now?" said my mum, looking at her watch. "It's only half-past two, and the bus doesn't go till six."

"Funfair again?" said Angela hopefully, and my heart sank. I didn't think my stomach would take another go on that Big Dipper when it was full of fried haddock and chips and bread and butter and coke.

My dad glanced down at Daniel, who was looking a bit bored and fed-up.

"I think we should give Daniel a good run," he said. "The poor chap's been on his lead all day. And it won't do any of us any harm to stretch our legs."

So I pulled my rucksack onto my back, and with my mum carrying the rabbit we set off along the coast path round the bay. Daniel was ecstatic to be off the lead, and it was good to be out in the fresh air after the hot, stuffy pub. Even Angela enjoyed the exercise, and raced about chasing Daniel and throwing sticks for him until they were both out of breath.

A stiff breeze was blowing and some sailing boats were scudding rapidly about in the bay. We stood on the clifftop watching them for a while, then Uncle Jim heaved a sigh.

"Pity we didn't manage a sail this holiday, Ted," he said regretfully. "A week just hasn't been long enough."

My dad pointed to a passenger cruiser chugging towards the headland.

"We could always have a trip on the old Skylark," he suggested. "It's not quite sailing, but it's better than nowt."

Angela flung her arms round her dad's middle.

"Oh, Dad! Do let's!" she cried. "It's our last chance before we go home!"

Auntie Sally looked at my mum doubtfully.

"I think it's going to rain," my mum said. "I can feel a few spots already."

"Don't talk daft, man," snorted my dad. "A bit of drizzle never hurt anybody."

But the mums weren't keen. "Leave us out of it," they said. "Just take the girls."

In the end that's what was decided. The two mums and Daniel went back to the bus station, because there was a tea-bar there where they could get a nice hot cup of tea and a hot cross bun. And Angela and I and our two dads walked down to the harbour to catch the last boat trip of the day.

The sea looked a bit rough, but we didn't mind. We clambered on board and found ourselves spaces on a wooden bench, and I stowed my rucksack in a locker behind Angela's feet.

"Heave-ho me hearties!" shouted my dad, his silly mood returning as soon as the crew cast off. "Shiver me timbers!" And I was dead embarrassed because everybody laughed and that made him show off even more.

"Abaft the beam!" he called out, and, "Ready

about, lee-oh!" and, "Yo-ho-ho and a bottle of rum!" and stuff like that, until I was almost ready to jump in the sea.

We left the harbour and chugged out across the bay, with the skipper's voice speaking through a loudspeaker and pointing out things of interest, like the cormorants and razorbills nesting on the cliffs.

"Isn't this great, Charlie!" beamed Angela, her eyes sparkling. "I love being on a ship. All we need now are some ship's biscuits."

"With the weevils going pop?" suggested my dad mischievously, and Angela gave him a puzzled look.

"Have you never heard of *Pop Goes the Weevil*?" laughed my dad, and Angela groaned and put her hands over her ears in despair.

All too soon the cruise was over and we began heading back towards the harbour. The grey clouds had been steadily turning black, and the rain, which had been threatening all day, now began to fall.

"Wow, we're going to get soaked!" said Angela, and she hurriedly put up the hood of her coat. My dad and Uncle Jim, busy chatting and joking with one of the crew, did the same.

"Quick, Angela! Pass my rucksack! My anorak's in it!" I said, as the rain began to soak through my sweater, so she bent down, opened the locker under the bench and dragged my rucksack out.

She stood up to pass it to me, and I still don't know to this day whether she really meant to do it, but somehow she managed to slip on the wet deck and stumble sideways so that the rucksack flew out of her hands and shot over the side of the boat into the sea.

I tried to grab it as it went over but I was too late. I kneeled on the seat and looked over the side, just in time to see the rucksack hit the water with a splash.

Angela knelt up beside me and together we watched it bob about for a moment on the waves. Then it filled with water and slowly sank from sight.

"Oooh Charlie!" she said, looking at me with a tragic face. "I am sorry!"

I watched the rucksack disappear. Then I turned and gave her a huge grin.

"It's OK, Angela," I said cheerfully. "I hated that old anorak anyway. The fishes are welcome to it."

She frowned and gazed out across the water, and I could see she was dead miffed that I wasn't more upset. But the best bit was still to come.

I put my hand on her arm.

"Pity about your blue silk jacket, though," I said, shaking my head sympathetically. "I don't suppose you'll ever get another one as nice as that."

"My WHAT?" she squeaked, her eyes opening wide in disbelief. "Charlie, don't tell me my BLUE JACKET was in THAT RUCKSACK!"

I put on a really sad face.

"I'm afraid so," I said. "I've been meaning to give it back to you all day."

I can't tell you what she said next, because it's too rude to write down, but if you imagine the rudest word you can think of you won't be far wrong. She went stomping off to the other end of the boat, and at the look on her face I couldn't keep my sad expression any longer. I just stood there in the pouring rain, laughing and laughing until I couldn't laugh any more.

And that was the last word she said to me on that holiday, because when we came off the boat I was soaked to the skin, and after giving my dad a good telling-off for not looking after me properly, my mum whisked me into the nearest shop and bought me not only a new sweater and jeans but a lovely new goldy-coloured anorak as well. I changed in the shop's changing room and put my wet clothes in a bag, so I was all snug and dry and warm for the bus ride home.

On the bus I offered Angela the orange rabbit to make amends, but she only looked at it with her nose turned up, as if the poor rabbit had just crawled out of a sewer, and she didn't speak to me at all.

That suited me just fine. I sat by the window with one arm round Daniel and the other round the rabbit, and as I watched the sky darkening and the street lights begin to twinkle in the rain I thought about the next eight days. There was still Easter Sunday to look forward to, and we were going to my gran's for the day. I was sure my grandad would have bought me a chocolate Easter egg, and even my mum might have been a bit extravagant this year, and bought me not only two pairs of socks from Marks and Spencers but a pair of knickers as well.

These were all good thoughts, but there was one even better. A thought that I savoured over and over again like a secret treasure. In just a few more hours, Angela would be on her way home.

# READ MORE IN PUFFIN

For children of all ages, Puffin represents quality and variety – the very best in publishing today around the world.

For complete information about books available from Puffin – and Penguin – and how to order them, contact us at the appropriate address below. Please note that for copyright reasons the selection of books varies from country to country.

**On the world wide web**: www.penguin.co.uk

**In the United Kingdom**: Please write to *Dept. EP, Penguin Books Ltd, Bath Road, Harmondsworth, West Drayton, Middlesex UB7 ODA*

**In the United States**: Please write to *Consumer Sales, Penguin USA, P.O. Box 999, Dept. 17109, Bergenfield, New Jersey 07621-0120*. VISA and MasterCard holders call 1-800-253-6476 to order Penguin titles

**In Canada**: Please write to *Penguin Books Canada Ltd, 10 Alcorn Avenue, Suite 300, Toronto, Ontario M4V 3B2*

**In Australia**: Please write to *Penguin Books Australia Ltd, P.O. Box 257, Ringwood, Victoria 3134*

**In New Zealand**: Please write to *Penguin Books (NZ) Ltd, Private Bag 102902, North Shore Mail Centre, Auckland 10*

**In India**: Please write to *Penguin Books India Pvt Ltd, 706 Eros Apartments, 56 Nehru Place, New Delhi 110 019*

**In the Netherlands**: Please write to *Penguin Books Netherlands bv, Postbus 3507, NL-1001 AH Amsterdam*

**In Germany**: Please write to *Penguin Books Deutschland GmbH, Metzlerstrasse 26, 60594 Frankfurt am Main*

**In Spain**: Please write to *Penguin Books S. A., Bravo Murillo 19, 1° B, 28015 Madrid*

**In Italy**: Please write to *Penguin Italia s.r.l., Via Felice Casati 20, I–20124 Milano*

**In France**: Please write to *Penguin France S. A., 17 rue Lejeune, F–31000 Toulouse*

**In Japan**: Please write to *Penguin Books Japan, Ishikiribashi Building, 2–5–4, Suido, Bunkyo-ku, Tokyo 112*

**In South Africa**: Please write to *Longman Penguin Southern Africa (Pty) Ltd, Private Bag X08, Bertsham 2013*